The Major,
the Poacher,
and the Wonderful
One-Trout River

DAYTON O. HYDE

The Major, the Poacher, and the Wonderful One-Trout River

"Give me but ten who are trout-hearted men!"
MAJOR GEORGE QUILLAINE
1919–

ATHENEUM 1985 NEW YORK

Library of Congress Cataloging in Publication Data

Hyde, Dayton O.
The major, the poacher, and the wonderful one-trout river.

SUMMARY: *The Major, who seeks to raise one record-*
breaking size trout, engages in a duel of wits with a
fourteen-year-old poacher at his trout stream.
1. Children's stories, American. [1. Trout—Fiction.
2. Fish culture—Fiction] I. Title.
PZ7.H9676Maj   1985   [Fic]   84-20442
ISBN 0-689-31107-9

Published simultaneously in Canada by
McClelland & Stewart, Ltd.
Composition by Heritage Press, Charlotte, North Carolina
Printed and bound by Fairfield Graphics, Fairfield, Pennsylvania
Designed by Mary Ahern
First Edition

The Major,
the Poacher,
and the Wonderful
One-Trout River

1

Like a big boar raccoon setting off on a foraging expedition after a long winter's sleep, Plummey Pittock rubbed his eyes, lowered himself through the trapdoor of his tree house in the top of the big cottonwood tree, and groped about in the damp, early-morning darkness until his bare toes touched a well-worn branch. His careful, bark-scuffing descent was made hazardous by the old, worn, wicker fishing creel banging on one hip, and his pop's trusty, rusty telescoping steel fishing pole carried strapped across his gaunt shoulders.

He held his cheapie pocket watch up before his eyes and strained to read the faded luminescence of the dial. It was getting late! He would have to scramble if he intended to beat that fancy fly-fisherman, Major Quillaine, to what Plummey considered his own proper family inheritance, the opening moment of trout season on what was known locally as the Great Pool of the Deschutes.

MAJOR GEORGE QUILLAINE sat ramrod straight in the front seat of his Jeep Wagoneer, toughing out the long frosty hours of early morning, but determined not to sleep through the opening moment of trout season. It was a point of honor that he should waft the first dry fly of the season over his favorite water, the Great Pool of the Deschutes.

Ever since *Sports Illustrated* had called him "King of the Flycasters," and the Museum of American Fly-fishing had reserved a special case for one of his flyrods, alongside rods of Zane Grey, Ernest Hemingway, and Bing Crosby, the public had resigned the opening hours on the famous pool to being the Major's very own.

It was the Major, after all, who had spearheaded the campaign to designate this stretch of the Deschutes "fly-fishing only." The bait fishermen had grumbled, but the Major had gotten his way.

Shortly before dawn, he squirmed into his rubber chest waders, swallowed a piece of cold venison sausage, swigged a businesslike draught of hot tea from his Thermos, pulled down his lucky L.L. Bean hat over his patrician forehead, zipped his laden fly vest up over his winter paunch, took up his delicate Orvis bamboo, a spare tip, plus three extra reels wound with three varied lines, then headed through early morning mists toward the Great Pool.

Overhead, a Wilson's snipe winnowed; skimming

the gun-metal gray surface of the river, a water ouzel carried an Odonata nymph to a bulky nest beneath a waterfall; a sandpiper sounded the first *peet-weet* of the new day.

It was part of his ritual that, regardless of the hatch, he start with a fly he'd made famous, a buff, bifurcated Baetis on a twenty-two hook, which Hooks Meyer himself had dubbed Quillaine's Quill. Pausing in the thickets, he tied one to a thin, silk leader, holding the tiny eyelet silhouetted against the rose of an emergent dawn so he could see.

Scattered wind clouds reflected a raspberry tint to the riffle below the pool, and the roaring chute at the head threw up rainbows of drifting spray.

"This is it, Quillaine," he murmured to himself. "The end of winter long!"

Heart pounding, he tiptoed forward, careful lest some tiny vibration from his footfall broadcast an alarm to the sly, wary denizens of the Pool. Touching the tiny Quillaine's Quill to his lips, he blew on it softly, partly to fluff the ginger hairs, partly for good luck.

"Gotcha!" a voice called out.

At the head of the pool, a young boy leaped from his rocky perch, his metal telescope rod creaking under the strain as a giant rainbow trout soared from the foam, attempted to shake the hook, and splashed *kerchunk* back into the torrent.

"Holy gerwollies! Ain't he a monster?" The boy giggled to himself.

5

The Major sagged against the bole of a cottonwood tree and slid earthward. His heart pounded fiercely, and pains shot through his chest. Someone had beaten him to the Great Pool! And—my God—a bait fisherman at that! Couldn't he read the signs? FLY-FISHING ONLY! He'd arrest that poacher, drag him before the courts. The death penalty would be too lenient; he'd suggest torture!

He tried to rise, but shock rendered him helpless. He tried to shout out blasphemies, but his jaws clenched like a bulldog's. Instead of a scathing outpouring, there was only a wet gurgle.

The huge trout made a spectacular series of frenetic leaps, trying to gain the swift water, but the boy, with his heavy wire leader, skidded him up on the wet sand and pinned him with a wrestler's leap. Desperately, the Major tried to raise himself on one elbow to get a look at the boy's face; but the poacher spotted motion, grabbed up his trophy by the gills, and sprinted for the brush, leaving only a battered Prince Albert can half-filled with night crawlers perched jauntily on a rock.

Slowly, the Major pulled himself to his feet. The Great Pool was ruined! Violated! He took the unused Quillaine's Quill between thumb and forefinger and stripped it off, placed it on his hat band, reeled up his line, took apart his rod, wiped it, placed it in its case, and trudged back to his car.

2

It was an accepted fact that nobody, and that means NOBODY, could dance a ginger quill on trout water like Major Quillaine. Such was the state of his art that often a natural would join his fly in an instant final love ballet, seconds before a lurking trout rose to gobble them both. If ever a mortal lived, ate, slept, and breathed fly-fishing, it was the Major.

At cocktail parties, you didn't move away at his approach, you RAN, or there you were trapped and conspicuous as a fly in cream; ice melted in what had been a drink; you were powerless to head for a refill, as he described wafting a fly he himself had designed, catching and releasing what had to be a record trout. And not a record for Deschutes County, Oregon; for all of North America!

According to Major Quillaine, life could never be termed "just" or "fair" until the best flycaster in America caught the biggest trout in America. It irked him that with fair frequency the record trout seemed to be taken by some sixteen-year-old "nothing" of a boy who thought a hatch had something to do with chickens and just happened to be dangling some indecent meat imitation like a bucktail coachman off a bridge at the proper moment when the record trout managed to snag himself by a protruding lip and run aground in an adjacent beaver run.

As to his own failure through the years to capture North American honors, he generally let it be known that during each season he'd released several fish larger than the champion, granting freedom as reward for a struggle nobly performed.

His chest waders he wore like a second skin. Six days after the disaster at the Great Pool, he came dragging in late to a dinner honoring a friend's anniversary, still garbed for wading, forced off the river by darkness. Completely at ease, he waddled like a rubber duck among his friends in evening attire. If a few trout scales happened to flake off and lie iridescent as pearls on the carpet, his friends were polite enough not to notice.

"Should have seen the big brookie I turned loose on the Upper Williamson the other day," he said, cornering a relative of the host. Stripping out imaginary line from an invisible reel, eyes glazing over, he turned his empty martini glass into a delicate bamboo rod.

"A hatch of midges was dancing when I arrived, but cold air settled off the hillside and the thermometer on my vest showed a drop of eight degrees in ten minutes. The action quit, of course. Dimple here; dimple there. I was about to call it a day when I noticed an interesting swirl some twenty yards downstream.

"What with a wind hard in my face, it was a deucedly difficult cast, but I tied on a ginger quill and managed to make it dance just ahead of the boil. Well, the biggest brookie in the world leaped up, slapped down my imitation with his flashing tail, and grabbed it before it hit the water. I tell you, the fight was on! That quarter-pound-test silk thread I borrowed once from the night dress of a duchess slashed the pool like a knife-fighter's Bowie."

Major Quillaine had been something called a hydrologist for the Federal Government, and his knowledge of trout streams was encyclopedic. After-hours from his job, he'd fished everybody's home stream. Tell him a boyhood yarn about fishing some brook flowing obscurely into the Chewaucan or the Yahooey, and if it had once held trout, he'd fished it, and let you know in his dead serious way that you'd presented the wrong flies, cast the wrong water, and everything you managed to take must have been foul hooked. Not that he wanted to put you down; at heart he was a teacher. He simply wanted you to do better next time.

The host's relative was about to escape to refill his glass, but the hostess, with a malicious gleam in her eye, drifted up to fill it for him from a silver pitcher. The poor man delved back into a boyhood in Wisconsin and came up with a stream the Major couldn't possibly have known about.

The Major's face lit up like a pinball machine.

"Aha!" he said. "Fished that stream on my twentieth birthday, in 'thirty-nine. Sixty-five now. Packed into a series of beaver dams at its head. Long gone now. In the 'forties they exceeded their food supply and moved on.

"One evening when the beaver were kerchunking out through the tunnels from their lodges, and the midges were singing so loud you couldn't have heard a raven on your shoulder, I took out a little Hardy fly pack containing some lovely English patterns. I remembered seeing one tied on a three X long shank to resemble a midge's larva. In short order I had it on a three foot leader the fairies must have woven from finest gossamer. I made that little love sink to the deepest waters of the beaver pond, then began to retrieve it with just the tiniest little reflex jerks of my partially bent knees.

"Suddenly, a monstrous brookie boiled from the depths, caromed off a sunken log for speed, took the midge on his lip, carried like a moon rocket into the air, then fell back to make such an absolute froth of the pond, I swear, we didn't see another beaver for a month!

"My mind's no good anymore," he complained, "or I'd tell you the name of the forester took me in there. Aha! Meyer Bardill! That's right. You know him? And his wife's name was—um—Liza. Five kids. Peter, John, Kitty, Annie, and Steve. Lord time flies. Steven will be fifty-five June first."

The Major's audience blinked and looked impressed, as though wondering if the Major ever forgot anything. "That's very interesting," the man from Wisconsin said, holding out his glass to the hostess for another refill.

The Major glanced across the room, as though to locate his wife, and went on with another story.

The Major's wife, Belle, was a stocky woman but cheerfully athletic, perfectly capable still of portaging her own canoe along Boundary Waters Wilderness trails, ignoring no-see-ums, making parfleche moccasins out of moosehide when hers wore through. Or turning out a seven course dinner from a Dutch oven beside a rain-drenched campfire. She was particularly adroit at sensing a fishing tale moments before it began, giving herself time to wander gracefully off to join another group.

The Quillaines had arrived at the party together and would depart thus, but the rest of the evening would shun each other like two magnets. Now, as the Major caught her eye across the room, it would have taken a sharp observer to catch Belle's faint smile as the Major took a sip of his drink, then deftly brought the conversation back to fishing, and maneuvered the biggest cutthroat trout ever taken from the Yellowstone to the shallows around his listener's feet.

It helped that Belle adored the Major. He was, after all, singular, an issue of one, for which the molds had been immediately broken, a hard-working, faithful, absolutely predictable man. As Belle returned the Major's glance, she was, at that moment, in a rare outburst of confidence, explaining to a friend that she loved knowing that two years from now or five, she would still be living with the Major in the same town, on the same street, in the same house.

Just six weeks after she made that statement, however, Belle was packing their things into pasteboard cartons as they prepared to move into an old farmhouse close to the mighty Deschutes River.

3

WHAT PRECIPITATED the move out of town was the fact that the Major had noticed that his ginger quill hadn't been rising for him quite so well lately. At first, he suspected a minute, hairline fracture of his fly rod; but when he could find no defects in his equipment, he turned to what for him was the court of last resort, his family physician, who detected just the tiniest bit of calcification in the shoulder joints, which might be slowing the Major's timing.

"Get along with it, Major!" The doctor snorted. "You've got the drive of a young man, and I don't want to see you in this office again until you're a hundred and ten!"

The ginger quill began to dance over the stream as before, but it took greater concentration. And for the first time in his life, the Major began to concern himself with posterity.

"You know, Belle," the Major said to his wife one night after dinner. "Before this, I've never really regretted that we haven't had children. It was one of those things. It occurs to me now, however, that I have no one to whom I can leave my fishing rods."

But it was his name in an exalted place in the record books that would have satisfied the Major more than an heir to carry on the Quillaine name. A dread of one day being forgotten began to irritate him like a cheatgrass seed in a woolen sock. It made for sleepless hours after midnight and a slight worsening of his disposition, though to see him striding down Main Street, half a step ahead of his cronies, he seemed still his old self.

For the Major, it was time to consider, in the privacy of his own thoughts, that he was growing older; and if ever he was to go down in the fishing Hall of Fame for taking the greatest trout in North America, he'd better be about it.

Finding that fish to catch was another matter. Checking out the fishing scene, he made a special sentimental pilgrimage to areas where once he had triumphed. Silver Creek in Idaho, then on to the Madison, the Green, the Kootenai, and Henry's Fork.

From there, he flew on to northern Michigan to renew a friendship with the Yellowdog, the Garlic, Maki's Marsh on the Laughing Whitefish, and the Two-hearted River; moved East to push himself nearly past endurance on the Battenkill and the Neversink. Quitting the Atlantic Seaboard, he headed north and west, sampling the Pancake, the Old Woman, and the best Canada had to offer.

North America's trout water, he decided, was polluted, crowded, and over-fished. The lonely vistas and secret big trout havens of his youth had either been altered by progress, polluted by acid rain, or so popularized by fishing editors that, if there was a place left in North America where that certain champion trout lay waiting, the Major could not guess where it could be.

It might even be too late. What really irked him was that all those years when he'd been discoursing about the big ones he'd caught and released, he'd been telling the truth. He'd caught fish that would have shattered records, but to quit fishing when a hatch was on was unthinkable; and to kill a noble trout, to have it weighed, measured, and certified for the record books was something his immense respect for his quarry would never let him do.

He came back from his travels convinced that there was but one option left him, and that would require selling his town house and finding that certain piece of property to take its place.

At his age, the decision to move came hard, and those who knew the Major well noticed that the man was not his old self. Someone pointed out that he had been back three days and had not once mentioned fishing.

"Hey, Maj," a churl at the local saloon called to him, emboldened by too much booze. "Tell us about the time you caught and released the big one down on the Klamath!"

There was a deathly hush in the barroom as though the Earps had just entered, guns loose in their holsters.

But the Major's mind was weighing potential real-estate transactions; he studied the bubbles in his glass of beer and let no outward change in his reflective mask show that he had even heard.

Clearly, the Major was pondering something of importance, but no one was able to guess what. When Friday Sites, the local woodcutter, saw the Major traveling afoot along the Deschutes plain, packing a small D-handled shovel, the in-joke was that the Major was digging angleworms; but when three of the Major's cronies rushed over, hoping to catch him in disgrace, the Major spotted them from afar and simply vanished into the tangles of live willow and dead flotsam north of the old Prince Mill.

Having shaken his pursuers, he emerged more than a mile upstream, on the Pittock Bottom, a lonesome, run-down ranch, where, years past, the rampaging Deschutes had deposited a collection of thin, gravelly soils and house-sized lava rocks over every acre. The last of the Pittocks had left the old ranchhouse to move up over the rim of the canyon to better, though not that much better, soils.

For a man unused to digging, the Major handled his shovel remarkably well. He dug hole after hole across the fields, satisfying himself that beneath the gravel lay a solid base of soil and clay.

From the ruin of the Pittock horse barn, he took an old amber liniment bottle half aslosh with what might have been the original fluid and commenced a primitive bit of engineering. By holding the bottle level on its side and sighting through it, then blazing trees with his pocket knife, he moved up the valley, determining the amount of fall from the bottom of the Pittock place to the top.

When, three days later, Friday, the woodcutter, let it be known about town that he had spied Belle on the front porch of the old Pittock house, looking grim and determined as she strong-armed a broom across warped and weathered boards, folks guessed what the local realtor had only hoped; that the Quillaines had decided to buy the place.

The town split wide open on the issue. Half the town thought the Major was losing his grip on reality; the other half thought the Major was up to something.

"Diggin' holes along the river, was he?" Big Ed Bentley quizzed Friday as he helped him fell an ancient juniper. "And then he upped and offered for the proppity?"

"Yep," Friday said. "Thought fer a while he was diggin' worms, but I guess he was just lookin' fer somethin' in the soil."

"Ef he looked at thet soil 'n' still bought the place," Big Ed said, thinking hard, "then he must hev dug up somethin' the rest of us don't know about. You reckon?"

"Major's a smart man," Friday said. "Been all over the world, he has. Idyho, Calyfornia, Washington State. All them places."

"Further'n thet even," Big Ed said. "Thet ain't the whole dang world, yuh know." A vague suspicion entered his mind and bloomed into an idea. "You stay here, Friday, an' cut 'er up into blocks. I gotta go to town 'n' git somethin' at the store."

"Stay here, my foot!" Friday said. "I'm goin' along. After all, I own the bicycle."

"Cold" Friese, the owner of the general store, sat on a bench basking in the hot summer sun. He grinned to himself as Big Ed and Friday came wobbling around the bend of the dusty gravel road, doubling up on Friday's old blue bicycle. Friday pumped, while Big Ed balanced on the tool rack over the rear tire.

"Hey, Maybelle," Friese called inside the store. "You want to see a sight? Come out here and look on down the road. And bring me a cream soda while you're at it."

"What can I do you boys out of today?" Friese said by way of greeting.

"Something we need from the store," Big Ed said. "Right, Friday?"

"Yeah," Friday said. "Sure hope you got them in stock."

The storekeeper's eyes twinkled. He knew what they were after. "So happens I'm fresh out," he said.

"All out?" Big Ed protested. "Hold on now. You don't even know yet what we—"

"Gold pans, right?" Friese grinned. "Had a dozen of them in stock for tourists, and sold every one of them today." He looked hard at Friday. "Seems somebody around here's been spying on the Major. Saw him digging along the river, then he upped and offered for that worthless old Pittock Bottom. The soil wouldn't raise a peck of spuds to the acre or enough grain to winter a blackbird. They figure the Major's a smart man, right? So they're guessing he must have found something in that gravel. Like gold!"

"Right!" Big Ed and Friday chimed in unison.

"Wrong!" Friese said, laughing. "Heck sakes," he scoffed. "No one could find gold on that bottom!" He took the bottle of pop from his wife and opened it as the two men turned their bicycle around and left.

"Gold!" Friese snorted to his wife as he took a swig. "Everybody knows there's no gold in this lava country. Still," he said, "I'm glad of two things."

"What things?" Maybelle asked.

"Glad I've got you to tend store. And glad I saved one of those gold pans back for myself. Like everyone says: that Major's a smart man!"

4

PURCHASING the Lower Pittock place turned out to be simple enough; the family had been waiting for a Major Quillaine to come along for years. But the Major had plans for the land that involved changes in patterns of historic water usage: from what had been simply irrigation of the rocky meadows for pasture to diverting the water into what the Major described only as a "planned, non-agricultural system of canals and waterways." At the state level, the changes were granted. The County Planning Department, however, reminded the Quillaines that whatever it was they contemplated had to be contrary to the law and could only be dealt with by applying for a variance.

Quillaine watchers, muscles sore from squatting along the Deschutes in fruitless search for gold, now turned their attention to the coming hearing; while another group, the D.A.P., Deschuters Against Progress, still not at all sure what the Major planned, began to organize local opposition.

It was not that the Major was against the law he wanted to violate. Many a time he had argued hard and eloquently against variances, since, at heart, he believed in wise, disciplined use of the land. But now his dreams were at stake, and he was determined that any restrictions on his changing the flows of irrigation waters from the Deschutes be dropped like a steaming teakettle with a wire handle.

The Major came flopping in with chest waders, a half-hour late for his own hearing. By then the opposition had already testified and were smirking with anticipated victory.

"Sorry I was late, folks," the Major said, "but there was a hatch on." He spotted an empty seat in the front row, rolled his chest waders back to his waist, then sat down on the lip of the seat, ready to take on all comers about an issue they shouldn't have commenced comment on in his absence anyhow.

As though part of a campaign to bring the audience over to his side and silence his critics, he fixed the crowd with frequent over-the-shoulder smiles, touching each of his cronies with a look of recognition, turning to cast an imaginary fly into their laps clear across the hearing room. Some people swore afterwards they could actually see a line sail out over the crowd and drop a midge right into a man's pocket. Pleased to be recognized by such a well-known man, each recipient of attention beamed pleasantly in his turn.

In the warm atmosphere of the hearing room, the damp chest waders began to steam. Watching the Major at work, the hearings officer concluded it to be the better part of wisdom to call the meeting into recess until the crowd settled, and the Major had been apprised of what had gone on before. But the Major forestalled him. Anxious to get back on the stream, he had already tallied his support and had even brought a few dissenters over to his side by giving each that warm, personal cast from the man so many considered to be the finest flycaster in America. A vote was taken, and one by one, the audience rose to his support and the variance was granted.

Elated, the Major gave the D.A.P. dissenters no time to grumble, ignored the chairman, and launched into a personally conducted tour of the great trout streams of America, including the Pimpernel and the legendary Caribou.

The Major might have gone on for half an hour, had not this glance lighted on a young boy in the back row who seemed vaguely, yet disturbingly familiar. For one long moment, the Major's jaw seemed to lock shut in a paralysis of concentration.

It was the chance the crowd had been waiting for; as a body, it rose to its feet to escape.

"You!" the Major shouted at the lad. "You Worm Fisherman! Stand where you are!"

"Congratulations, Major," someone said, pumping his hand.

"Great show, Major," another man said.

When the Major was finally able to wrench his hand loose, the boy had fled.

5

PLUMMEY PITTOCK hung by his knees from a cottonwood limb and looked out over the fields. Today was
Sunday, and all day he was going to be Tarzan of the
Apes. Upside down, the trees and bushes seemed to grow
from the sky and the shining Deschutes to cradle them
from horizon to horizon with a silver ribbon.

A great orange and black caterpillar walked along
the underside of a leaf, pausing now and then to lift its
fore half out into dizzying space, as though trying to
bridge the gap between the leaf and Plummey's nose.

Up (or down) past his knees, he could glimpse his
big tree house, solidly anchored in a massive hand of
limbs, hidden from the world by silvery green foliage.
An orange and black Bullock's oriole clung to its topsy
turvy nest, swaying in the light summer breeze. Today,
he, Tarzan, was going to spy on Major Quillaine, who
had bought the old Pittock bottom from his Grandma's
estate. Already, with the ink hardly dry on the purchase

contract and the variance, the Major had moved in some big tractors and earth-movers, lots bigger than the man would need to farm. He had listened in at the hearing, but never did figure out what it was the Major intended to do. He would have to spy on him; then, if the Major meant harm, Tarzan must warn all the animals in the jungle.

"Hey kid! What's your name?" The Major's voice boomed at him from the grass green sky. The enemy had slipped up on Tarzan from behind.

"Kid?" Plummey gurgled. "Me not Kid. Me Tarzan of the Apes, King of All the Birds and Animals in the Jungle!"

"Well, get down out of there, Tarzan, before that branch breaks, along with your fool neck! And what's that pile of boards you got up there? Looks like a pack rat's nest! This is my private property, and I want that junk cleaned out of there."

"This not your land! This land belong Tarzan of the Apes!" The boy swung right side up, grabbed a short rope dangling from an upper branch, and sailed out gracefully into thin air, landing catlike on a higher branch.

The Major was carrying a pack of no trespassing signs. He took one now and hammered it to the bole of the giant cottonwood with four aluminum nails.

"You coming down, kid, or do I have to climb up after you?"

On the upper side of the trunk, a short, wooden

24

ladder led up to the first branches of the tree. As Tarzan stuck out his tongue, the Major's eyes burned with the cold fury of a man who has never raised any children. He flung down his pack of signs and started up.

"Watch that third rung!" Tarzan shouted down at him.

Too late! The rung broke under the Major's weight, sending him crashing back to the hillside duff.

"Told ya," Tarzan muttered, leaping to a higher branch.

Clutching his arthritic shoulder, the Major glared upwards and tried again, carefully stepping past the broken rung.

"I can't believe some people," Tarzan of the Apes, alias Plummey Pittock, said, peering down at the grown-up climbing his tree. Well, Tarzan was set for invaders. Just as the Major reached the first tier of branches, the boy reached out and pulled a short rope. Above the Major, a five gallon grease bucket turned on an axis, dumping its rusty load of rain water on the man's head.

Sailing out over Major Quillaine, Tarzan let out a great cry of victory and landed still higher in the tree.

"You!" the Major sputtered, his face dark with rage. "I'll get you yet!" He groped for his worst epithet and spat it out. "You danged little bait fisherman!"

Tarzan moved a little higher. For an old man, the Major was scrambling up the tree remarkably well.

"Don't touch that branch, Mister!" Tarzan called down.

The Major ignored the advice and had barely placed his boot on the weathered stub when it shattered under his weight and left him clutching the rough bole of the old cottonwood with a desperate bear hug.

"Woodpecker hole on the far side," Tarzan explained.

While the Major's life was passing before his eyes, the boy used the diversion to scramble up through the trapdoor in the floor of the tree house and bolt it behind him.

From below came a ripping sound as the weakness of age and the forces of gravity combined to overcome the Major. He began to slide, leaving part of his L.L. Bean chamois cloth shirt hanging from a branch.

Content that he had defeated his enemy, Tarzan of the Apes picked up a batch of small trout he had caught on worms early that morning on the river and began to fry them in a pan over a small camp stove.

He had won the battle; and he would win the war too, when the Major went storming into the real estate office and discovered that the big cottonwood tree was not on his property after all, but on a corner of a piece of land extending up over the rimrocks where Plummey lived with his mother, a desolation of rocks and small fields known as the Upper Pittock.

He wished he could see the Major's face when he determined that the Upper Pittock had been left to Plummey in trust by his doting grandmother, and it would be another seven years before Plummey was twenty-one and could dispose of the property at will.

6

_____

FOR MAJOR QUILLAINE, the news at the real estate office was a shocker. He was a private man, cherishing his moments as a solitary fisherman on Life's stream. Surrounded by rimrocks shutting out the ugliness of civilization, the Pittock Bottom had seemed perfect for his needs. Now, right at the edge of his property was a lookout tower of a cottonwood tree, manned by a snoopy kid in a tree house, who would grant him few unwatched moments.

He remembered now seeing the kid often enough. Up and down the Deschutes from the time he was barely high enough to peer over a pumpkin, packing an old rusty steel telescoping rod with red garnet guides looking like rubies in the sun. In his mind he had shut the boy out, never even bothering a nod of greeting. It was not within the Major's capabilities to admit that in such a manner he had begun his own fishing experience, or that in Plummey, but for a span of some fifty odd years, went young Georgie Quillaine.

The Major seriously considered abandoning his project, or, at least, putting it on hold until, one day, the old cottonwood succumbed to the ravages of time, or the boy outgrew his interest in the tree house. But one night, as the Major lay sleepless, he heard the ticking of the old Seth Thomas clock and felt a sense of time passing by. He got up quietly from Belle's side, careful not to wake her, put on his robe, and went in to where he had set up his old ink-stained drawing boards, which had served him many a year, swiveled his chair to a comfortable height, and sat staring at a blank sheet of drawing paper until he achieved a quiet, sure sense of what he was about.

For several days, he toiled long into the night, laying out the land in purple ink, drawing careful, meticulous lines, and as often as not, relegating the entire work to the trash bin.

Belle tiptoed about, making the house habitable. If she bothered the Major at all, it was to bring him a cup of soup or tea, or run a caressing hand lightly across his shoulders as though to say, "I know your dream."

What the Major was attempting to design was the perfect trout environment, a faithful recreation of the greatest pools and riffles he had ever fished, and right in his own back yard. A series of spectacularly beautiful falls, rapids, and swirling deeps, weeded areas in just the proper proportion to produce a balanced cover and a rich food supply, varied, yet not so abundant so as to over-power the system. An aesthetic rendering of land and water, creating a fishery more productive and beautiful than anything Nature had yet managed.

At the upper end of the property, he designed a diversion point, carefully screened and regulated, where he could lead just the right amount of water in from the Deschutes, pass it through warming ponds until it attained the perfect temperature, then move it by gravity down through his system, picking up oxygen, gathering wastes, and passing out again into the Deschutes through screens at the lower end of his property. A closed system, into which no wild fish could enter, and from which no captive fish could escape.

In his long career as a hydrologist, he had kept his eyes open, storing up information toward what had then been only a vague sort of dream. Now, for hours on end, he sat in his darkened study, flashing color transparencies on a screen. A hauntingly beautiful pool on the Battenkill, beloved of artists; riffles on the Laughing Whitefish below Deerton; weedy, insect-producing areas on Silver Creek. If he had released those champion trout, he had returned to photograph those pools and riffles where he had caught them; now he sat quietly, reliving the moments and analyzing the conditions that had made those great fish possible.

After long, silent periods of contemplation, he would carefully take up his drafting implements once more and build a blueprint of what might one day approach perfection. Excitement pounded in his veins; he was creating the ultimate fishing river, a summation of great parts that would surely surpass anything Nature had managed.

Often on a moonlight night, he would rise from his bed excited by an idea and move out over the fields, drinking in the feel of the land, letting his imagination improve on Nature, then imprinting the finished scene hard and fast on his memory for morning.

So involved was he with his work that he almost forgot the old cottonwood tree, until, one day, as he checked out his boundary lines, he found a surveyor's corner hidden in a thicket of wild rose not far from the tree. It was a matter of inches, but the boy and the realtors had been correct; the cottonwood tree was just over the line, off the Major's property. And wishing wouldn't do a thing to move the tree.

He had forgotten all about the no trespassing sign he had nailed on the tree; and now, intent on taking it down, he stepped over the invisible line as though stepping over a snake. But as he reached for the sign, he drew back his hand. The boy had scratched out the Major's name and written in his own, Plummey H. Pittock, followed by a crude skull and crossbones.

As he followed his property line up the hillside toward the gray, lichen-encrusted rimrocks, he stumbled and went down the talus slopes on his rump, tearing his good, anti-snag, birdshooter britches and losing a bit of hide in the process. He could have sworn he heard someone giggle from the leafy palace high above, but when he looked up angrily, he could see no one.

A down-draft, however, brought the delicious smell of trout fried in butter, and when he passed under the tree again, half an hour later, a hand appeared over the side of the treehouse platform, and the skeletal framework of a large trout, picked clean, fell at his feet.

From the thick foliage of the cottonwood, he heard the Bullock's oriole scolding him as an interloper. A board in the treehouse creaked, and the Major landed with a leap back on his own property.

7

PLUMMEY LAY flat on his stomach, sprawled across the porch of his tree house, chin cradled on his fist, and watched the mysterious activity below. Neither rhyme nor reason to any of it. The din from the heavy equipment was awful, and he could feel the earth tremble right up here in the high reaches of his cottonwood perch. Dust rose in clouds to settle on everything from his dishes to the tip of his freckled nose.

First a huge, track-laying tractor would slam its bulldozer blade against a heavy stinger protruding from the rear of an earthmover, shoving the mover forward as a cutting edge dropped down to plane dirt into a big central maw. Then, when the bowl spilled over, the rubber-tired machine would clang shut, rise up higher on its wheels, and speed away to dump its load elsewhere, while another earthmover took its place at the burrow area.

Three times as Plummey watched, the Major was

almost squashed like a bug by giant tires as he rushed back and forth afoot, set up his transit, peered at wooden grade stakes, directed traffic, and signaled each operator where to load and where to dump.

The boy tried to figure it all out. If the Major planned to put in a crop of oats or alfalfa along his canals and irrigate, then he should be smoothing the land instead of tearing it up. And that rocky, horseshoe shaped ledge, which surfaced right in the middle of the field like a dinosaur's back and would have discouraged most farmers, only seemed to delight the Major, who shut down the earthmovers while he surveyed around the outcropping and set his stakes anew to accommodate the rocks.

Little by little, a pattern was taking shape. The Major had to be building the crookedest irrigation canal ever seen in the west. And the most impractical. He seemed more interested in irrigating rocks, ignoring the few areas of farmable soil. And the groves of young aspens and pines that had sprung up after his grandfather grew too old to farm—the dumb Major was protecting them as though they were sacred. Anybody knew you couldn't raise a crop with trees sprouting everywhere.

More activity. A flatbed truck laden with two big black cast iron head gates churned across the dusty field, followed by a convoy of concrete trucks, their big cargo bowls turning, mixing concrete as they drove. When they moved out of sight around a bend in the rimrocks, the boy could stand it no longer. Scampering down his cottonwood like a bee-stung bear, he ascended the rimrock and jogged along it, leaping from rock to rock until he gained a new vantage point overlooking the trucks.

The old diversion point his grandfather had used to take irrigation water from the Deschutes lay in shambles. The redwood gates and chutes, which had resisted decay for so many years and braved many a spring flood, had been ripped away, and in their place stood an imposing array of wooden forms for concrete.

Plummey perched comfortably on a lava rock and watched as a mobile crane set the heavy black head gates in position. If he didn't understand the rest of the operation, he did this. It was well planned. One giant head gate to let in water from the big river and another gate set a few yards down the ditch bank to allow excess water to escape back into the Deschutes. Below the head gates were an ingenious set of fish screens, designed, it seemed, to prevent even the tiniest minnow from entering the canal from the main river.

"Fair enough," Plummey thought critically. "But just wait until Mr. Beaver moves in and clogs up the works with debris. It'll take a grown man with a trash fork full time just to clean the screens."

But the Major had thought of that too. Just upstream, in the throat of the diversion, Plummey saw a giant waterwheel, the likes of which he had never imagined. Powered by river currents, it was set at an angle so that as it turned, giant screens rotated like a Dutch windmill and filtered the water of all trash, carrying even the smallest twig aloft, and side-delivered it back into the main current.

The Major had ridden up the canyon on the running board of the lead truck, although he might have walked it faster. Now he stepped down and took charge, signaling the first big concrete carrier back into position. Soon its sloppy gray cargo flowed down a delivery chute into the waiting wooden forms, while men with shovels and small portable vibrators settled the "mud" into place, working it far down into trenches jack-hammered into bedrock, where winter frosts could not heave the structure out.

It was almost dark when the last of the concrete had been poured and the works covered with straw, so that the concrete would harden slowly and well. As Plummey stood on the rimrock and watched the last truck depart empty, he heard in the distance the dinner horn his mother used to summon him in to eat. He was hungry. So absorbed had he been in watching the Major's operation, he had forgotten to eat lunch.

The lights from his mother's little house across the rock flats twinkled like fireflies, guiding him home.

"Plummey, dear," his mother said as she set a large, steaming bowl of black bean soup before him. "I hope you didn't spend your day spying on the Major."

"Who, me?" Plummey said, feigning innocence. He could hardly wait for morning when once more he could man his spy station high in the old cottonwood, to watch what the Major was about.

8

By no stretch of the imagination could Major Quillaine be called rich, but he had a comfortable retirement from years as a government hydrologist and had managed to do some moonlighting along the way for some notable clients who had been more than grateful. For instance, there were the salmon pools he had designed in Scotland for the Earl of D-, breathtaking in natural beauty, as well as biologically and hydrologically superb.

"Designed for fish by a genius who must be half fish himself," said the Earl, slipping a check for several hundred pounds into the pocket of Major Quillaine's shooting vest.

There was a trout stream in Quebec, owned by a famous fishing club, a lovely piece of water but sterilized by acid rain from the industrial plants in the cities. It hadn't taken the Major long to recognize the problem and restore the ph to optimum, by hiring a bulldozer to remove a deposit of sediment and bare a substrate of limestone. Some of the members had been grateful enough to make a few quiet little investments in their companies in Major Quillaine's name.

And then, of course, there was that bit of property on Silver Creek in Idaho, willed to him by a famous writer with whom he had shared a few little fly fishing secrets. The Nature Conservancy had acquired neighboring properties, and now his little piece had some real worth.

Through his lawyer, the Major now offered the Idaho piece to young Pittock. He would lease the Idaho property gratis to the Pittocks until young Plummey became twenty-one and could trade the Upper Pittock and his cottonwood tree for the Idaho land.

Even though the Silver Creek gem appraised out as being worth several times those rocky Pittock flats and juniper benches, Idaho seemed like the end of the world to a family that had lived for four generations along the Deschutes.

"It's hard to move to a crick," Plummey told his mother, "when all your life you've lived on a river."

Quietly and firmly, they said "no" to the plan.

The Major, of course, didn't understand their decision, but there was nothing he could do. He avoided even looking at the cottonwood tree, but busied himself with his project.

Even though Major Quillaine had cannily designed his system to utilize ancient stream channels and thus cut earth-moving expenses without compromising quality, he was forced to keep a tight rein on costs to avoid running over his slender budget. As the weeks went by, the construction workers acquired a healthy respect for the old man's abilities. Let a slope be off grade a cat's whisker, and they did the job over again on their own time.

Daytimes, the Major kept himself busy setting grade stakes and supervising men and machines. Far into the night he sat at his desk thumbing through catalogues, comparing prices, and writing out orders. Soon hardly a day went by without a call from the freight office, the airport, or United Parcel about arriving packages. Belle ran a ferry service. There were seeds, plants, and biological specimens shipped in from all corners. Phragmites to control erosion, hardstem bullrush, bur reed roots for marshy areas, white water lilies and lotus for fish cover. Wild rice, sweet flag, smartweed, elodea, and coontail. Bushels of lemna for quiet waters. Gallons of fairy shrimp, tadpoles, pond snails, water fleas, crayfish, and the larval forms of several species of aquatic insects.

All these arrivals had to be cared for in a temporary wetlands nursery until the time came to introduce them to the new system.

Belle rallied to his dream. In her house in town she'd been known for the earliest crocus, the finest tulips, daffodils, iris, roses, daylilies, and delphinium. Now she threw her energies into the Major's project. She could glance at the great blueprint on the wall of his office and visualize that the tubers she patiently heeled into mud would one day be replanted to become a raft of water-lilies, turning their flat pads up into the wind; that the sweet flag and camas would extend the blue of "water" back into green meadows, and the wild rice would soon nod gently along new backwaters as though it had been there always.

To the Major's plans, she added a special touch of her own. Islands of wild roses beneath ponderosa pines, buttercups, Indian paintbrush, meadow gentian, blue-eyed grass, and polemonium in the wet meadows. Wild strawberry and blueberry on the sandy edges. Wild gardening instead of tame. If she had been content in town, now her life took on new purpose, and her face a new radiance.

"Belle," the Major said one day. "You sure look better than you usually look!"

His wife shot him an inquiring glance, and perhaps overcome by his own tenderness, he blurted out, "You know, you're getting to be pretty as an Eastern brook trout in spawning time!"

Another wife might have bridled at the comparison, but Belle had seen those trout. Orange and crimson on creamy bellies. Fire opal colors. Coming from the Major, she knew it to be a compliment of the highest order.

The Major and his crew helped with the heavier chores of rototilling meadows and seeding in natives, but they were soon busy removing the forms from the concrete structures, while she worked on steadily, running tractors herself, bending, kneeling, digging, planting, until every bush, every tree, every seed destined for the higher areas was in the ground.

There was a brief cloud of blue smoke at the head of the valley as the Major set fire to the shattered form lumber and turned it into gray ash. That afternoon, the earthmovers finished up the lower end of the system with a quiet pool and a six-foot waterfall, which would one day deliver the borrowed water back into the Deschutes. The Major himself supervised the placement of the screens along the lip of the falls, which would prevent fish from gaining access to or escaping from the system.

"We're finally ready," the Major said quietly, as he paid off the last of the crew and watched the big machines go lumbering off down the road toward town. He sat down on a big rock along the road, did some figuring in his notebook, and admitted that he had brought off the whole job a week earlier than ever seemed possible and a thousand dollars under budget.

Elated, he took Belle by the hand, and together they walked up the dry, dusty streambed. Now and then, the Major would stop to work his way along the bank, trying a few imaginary casts, explaining his creation.

"Over there, for bright days, there'll be a deep backwater, and, come evening, the trout will move left to a long, gentle riffle to feed. In June, there will be a black drake hatch along that bank; in July, big yellow mays will drive the fish mad; in August, grasshoppers will drop from the tall canary grass bending over the stream banks. We've done it, Belle, girl! It's what I've dreamed of all my life: the perfect trout stream!"

At last, they moved through groves of aspen and tall yellow pines to the head of the system. The Major stood with his hands cradled over the massive iron wheel controlling the head gate. "Shall we turn it on?" he asked, trembling in his excitement.

"Let's," Belle said, her eyes dancing.

The heavy control wheel squawked for lack of grease as it threaded down its shaft and lifted the giant head gate in its housing, while from somewhere up the river a lovesick bittern answered hopefully. There was a gurgle beneath them as clear, crystal water from the Deschutes began to rush down the dry virgin barrens of the new channel.

It was tempting to turn in too much water too soon and risk eroding the delicate soils along the system. He settled on a stream of only a quarter of capacity, then sat with his wife as nighthawks boomed in the gathering dusk, watching as the new stream puddled and soaked up thirsty earth, then overflowed its basins to speed on into the next before finally disappearing around the first bend.

Plash! Plash! Plash! As the current swung into the system, the giant trash-catcher began to turn its windmill arms, and the screens filtered the inflowing water and delivered leaves and pine needles as well as other debris, back into the main river.

Slowly the moon came up over the rimrocks, looking impossibly large, to build a golden pathway across
the upper pool to the feet of the couple, as though beck-
oning them to cross.

"We built that bridge of gold, Belle," the Major
said softly. "In all of time, it was never there before!"

9

PLUMMEY BAITED an Eagle Claw snelled hook with a big fat yellow wood-borer grub he'd found in a rotten log, clinched a couple of big lead sinkers onto the line with his teeth, and cast out into the current, watching intently as the sweep of the Deschutes caught the bait and swept it right where he wanted it, back under the cutbank.

He kept one eye peeled for the law. Thanks to Major Quillaine, this section was fly-fishing only; but heck, he'd been born on this stretch of river. To his old man, it had been a case of fish and hunt or starve out. And so he had raised a family on trout and venison. To Plummey, the rules had been set by folks somewhere else, who hadn't bothered to consult him about what he wanted. Big city folks that fished the Deschutes for sport and didn't know what it felt like to be hungry.

His mom had said he could spend the night in the tree house, and a fat rainbow would go good for supper.

At the far edge of the pool, a spotted sandpiper trotted along a mossy log, calling nervously.

Plummey grinned. *"Peet weet! Peet weet!"* he whistled between his front teeth.

It was a mistake. A few yards up the gravel bar from where he fished, four tiny bits of fluff, almost perfectly camouflaged against the washed river rock, broke cover and trotted down the bank toward him. Crying plaintively, wingtips almost touching the stream, the mother flew toward her babies, landing on the bar, trying desperately to lead them away from danger. In the nearby willows, a black and white magpie laughed at their predicament with raucous voice and watched from a hidden perch to do them harm.

Plummey stood very still, but the tiny mites had already taken a shine to him, piling over his wet sneakers as though they were sticks of bleached driftwood. Afraid they would get stepped on, or be carried away by the magpie, he set his rod down on the rocks and bent to catch them up in his big, gentle hands. Not much bigger than his thumbnail, he let them snuggle a moment for warmth, then carried them across the bar and set them down in some clumps of joint grass where they would be safe.

"Peet weet! Peet weet!" the mother called, bobbing up and down in her anxiety. She flew to the far end of the bar and did a broken wing act, trying to lead him away. When Plummey moved back down the bar, she slipped on over to the grass, and the hatchlings left cover, trotted over to her, and followed her to safety.

When the boy looked back to where he had left his rod, he saw it skidding across the gravel, towed by a fish. He caught it just as it slid into the shallows, pulled it dripping from the water, and braked the clacking reel with his thumb. A heavy trout bowed the tip and sped away, making a run for a snarl of roots submerged in the stream.

Plummey held the fish up just short of the stump, then made him battle the current to use up strength. Again and again, the fish tried to head downstream with the current, but Plummey brought him about, keeping him under tight control. As he eased the fish closer to the surface, Plummey caught a flash of silver and pink. A rainbow. From the look he'd go four pounds or better. A good meal for supper, and there'd be plenty left over for his mom.

At Plummey's motion, the rainbow spooked and made a wild, splashing run away from him, disappearing into the dark shadows beneath the cutbank from which it had come. There it sulked and the boy thought for sure the fish had snagged the leader on a root. He pulled first one way then the other, expecting any moment to come up with a slack line. He had almost given up, when the trout came loose and rushed across the river, heading right toward him, throwing slack in the line.

The fish might easily have won its freedom had not its rush carried it up into the shallows; there, as the hook pulled from the rainbow's lip, Plummey rushed forward, batting his quarry out on the gravel bank.

Breaking off a willow fork, he inserted one fork

through the gills, and hoisting the heavy, flopping prize over his shoulder, he took his outfit and climbed the bank. He cut directly across the Major's property, keeping to the brushy areas as he headed toward the landmark cottonwood tree.

Coming up out of a swale thick with wild currant bushes, he almost collided with the Major and his wife, who were intent on raking seeds into the bare soils of the channel. Plummey dropped flat on his belly, holding the fish beneath him lest it make one last flop and alert the Quillaines.

"Whew!" he breathed in relief as they moved away without discovering he was there. "That was sure a closie!"

Rising to his feet, he grabbed his plunder and scurried across the bare waterway into the grove of aspens on the far bank. Under cover once more, it was easy to move undetected to the base of his tree. After hooking the fish to a rope, he climbed up to his tree house and pulled his catch on up after him.

When he looked again out over the fields, he saw that the Major and his wife had returned for more seed and discovered his tracks in the dust. Obviously, the Major was not pleased. He raised one arm, shook his fist in Plummey's direction, and might have rushed the tree had not the woman taken his arm.

Once, long after he had eaten a tasty supper and stretched out in his bedroll on the deck of his tree house, he heard voices in the fields. The Major's, followed by the woman's. Plummey wondered what was going on. He'd made a mess of the old place, the Major had. That was the problem when city people tried to become farmers.

That irrigation canal, for instance. Why it was so crooked in some places it almost met itself coming back. Made no sense; no sense at all. He could hardly wait until the Major turned water down the new ditch and tried to irrigate the land. Might be a smart man, the Major, but he sure wasn't practical. Wasted a lot of time and money on a system that any fool could see wasn't going to work. Why the whole length of the farm, there wasn't a single place where one could shove water out over the land and irrigate.

Several times during the night, Plummey thought he heard the gurgle of running water, but dismissed it as a sound carried on the wind from the Deschutes. But in the morning, as he raised up on an elbow, he stared out over the land, rubbing his eyes in amazement, then leaped to his feet.

Looking as though it had been there always, a lovely river wound down through what had once been the Pittock bottom. So that was it! The Major had built himself a trout stream! And what a beauty it was! From his perch, Plummey could see riffles, pools, waterfalls, shining ribbons of quiet water, and roaring white water chutes. The boy hugged himself in excitement; he could hardly wait until the Major stocked the new river with trout!

10

ALL NIGHT LONG, the Major tended his new river. For a time, he tried resting on a bed of pine needles under a gnarled and twisted tree near the head gate, listening to the rush of water through the fish screens, the regular *plash, plash, plash* of the trash-catcher, and the occasional hooting of a horned owl. But excitement buoyed him up, driving out his fatigue, and once again he was on the prowl, probing up and down the banks with his flashlight, seeking to cure small problems with adverse currents before they became big ones.

In the morning, when he decided that the river was running smoothly and there were no problems with erosion, he opened the head gate wide and let a full head of water move on down the channel, noting with satisfaction that the water flowed clear and silt-free over the gravelly bottom. Siltation was a major enemy of any trout stream, and the Major had taken painstaking care that the swiftest currents made their way over cobbles rather than fragile soils.

He gave the water sufficient head start to fill the system, then took his rod, tied on a light Cahill, and began to work his way down stream. There were no fish, of course, but he was eager to try out the currents and the varying personalities of each chute, each riffle, each pool.

His concentration was fierce, making mental notes to himself of where a sunken log was needed and at what angle to alter the flow, or where a rocky point needed to be extended to form a cutbank along an otherwise plain shore.

At times, he pulled a small blue notebook from a shirt pocket and sketched in changes, mapped out currents, or recorded water temperatures. He knew exactly where the fish would one day lie to take a certain hatch, or where they would seek out cover in the heat of a summer's day.

"Perfect!" he would exclaim with satisfaction, or "Splendid!" Now and then when he came across a series that had turned out particularly well, he might grade the run, "Perfectly splendid!"

He had progressed nearly half the way down through the fields when he came upon Belle, planting columbines in the cool of an aspen grove. She laid down her bucket and trowel and came to watch.

"How goes it?" she asked.

"A touch of Heaven." He grinned.

He held out the handle of the rod to her, but it was a token gesture. She knew from experience that no one, not even the Major's wife, dared touch that rod. And if she were to take it and cast, she would only down-grade their relationship. Her skill would never come up to the Major's expectations.

Just once, on their honeymoon trip, angling for Atlantic salmon in Labrador, she had tried fishing, and, by catching the largest fish, had ruined the Major's day. He had almost sent her packing.

Now she waved him on, seating herself to rest on a weathered log, her wide-brimmed hat across her stout knees. How easy he made it look! Behind him, the line flowed back over the meadow in a graceful curve, vanished as it shot forward out and over the stream, back again over the meadow, gathering force, then for-ward again to pause in midair as the fly floated gently down on the water with scarce a dimple. Again and again he cast, absorbed in his work, and she knew—but understood—that he had completely forgotten her pres-ence.

Resplendent in rusty plumage, a cinnamon teal came winging up the stream, flying low to investigate new territories. He landed with a shower of spray right in the Major's pool, almost running afoul of his line. The man smiled as the teal leaped into the air and veered away. Here was confirmation! The stream did actually exist!

Yet there was a dreamlike quality to the day's ex-perience; in a sense the river was not real but a recon-struction of the highs of his life. Here, on one pool, he was back on the Laughing Whitefish, fishing below

Mushrat John's, fifteen years old but already casting a long fly. A Parmacheene Belle, teased across a sunken log, had brought a huge trout arching into the air with the gaudy red and white Belle riding high on its lip.

Now came a series of rock runs and pools from the Lamoille. His uncle, Mac Drennan, had taken him out to teach him some basics and had ended up sitting on a log muttering to himself as George had out-fished the regulars. A black gnat, drifting dry down a chute, had taken the largest rainbow of the day. Another lad his age might have taken the trophy home to show; but even then, he had no truck with killing. Before his uncle could approach, George reached down quietly, wet his hands, and slipped the hook from the trout's lip.

Next, down the magic stream came a deep emerald steelhead pool on the Rogue, the despair of many a fishing guide, until, one day, a young Lieutenant Quillaine, on furlough from the Army, had unlocked its secrets.

Belle was not the only one that morning who watched. High on his eagle's roost, Plummey Pittock lay down his book to snoop. Dumb old Major! He ought to know there weren't any fish in that stream. What was he casting for? What a waste of effort. Maybe the old man's elevator had gotten off on the wrong floor, or he had lost his marbles.

But, suddenly, as Plummey became engrossed in watching; he forgot that the river had only been there since yesterday. He sat suddenly upright, half expecting a giant trout to take the Major's fly. He had never really watched the Major cast before. Now it hit him that in all his life he had never seen a sight more beautiful. Graceful! Controlled! There wasn't an instant when the fly left its trained, orderly orbit. A shiver of excitement electrified Plummey's thin body. Some day he was going to cast like that! Some day he was going to beat the Major at his own game!

He lay trying to figure out how the Major was doing it. It all seemed so effortless, but it had to come from long practice. That was it!

Even now, the Major wasn't trying to catch fish, he was practicing! Plummey hadn't paid much attention at the time, but suddenly he remembered someone talking about the Major, calling him the greatest flycaster in America. Wow!

He sat up straight so he could see better. First off, of course, he'd have to get a better rod than the old steel bait rod his father had left him. Often he had dreamed over the gleaming creations of fiberglass, graphite, and boron down at the store. The Major used a bamboo, and that cost a fortune! He had trouble even dreaming of it; what little money he put together from odd jobs around town, he gave to his mom. Somehow he had never wanted much for himself. The necessaries, like a good pocket knife and hone. Fishing tackle. Arrows. A guy could never have enough of them. And a bicycle! A guy needed wheels. But now, for the first time in his life, he had a real desire; and as long as he was just dreaming, then why not hanker for a bamboo rod just like the Major's.

Major Quillaine moved downstream to a new series. For a moment, he stood regarding the torrent plunging over the rocky horseshoe, then slipped quietly back from the stream, circling carefully as though afraid to disturb the pool. Plummey saw him stop to replace his fly. Then, without fanfare, he began to cast, paying out the line until fisherman, rod, line, leader, and fly all seemed part of a perfect flow.

Plummey got to his feet. A slight wind played in the top of the cottonwood; looking up against the moving clouds made him dizzy. From the oriole nest he heard baby bird sounds as a parent fed a nestful of young. Somewhere, maybe in the dusty storeroom over Goodrich's Emporium, he had seen what had to be the makings of a bamboo fly rod. Under some dusty boxes he had been carting out for Mr. Goodrich, he had found a tube of triangular strips of cane, just waiting to be worked. If only he could talk Mr. Goodrich out of those pieces, maybe he could make his own rod!

He started to sweep out his tree house, but the vision of those strips of bamboo grew too exciting for him to handle. Swinging down from his perch, he set off for his house, where he delivered the remains of the trout to his mother, took his bicycle, and rode on into town.

11

Not since the Major had taken a record thirty-pound Atlantic salmon from the Vididalsa in Iceland had he been so excited. It was time to add life to his stream, to introduce breeding stocks of a host of creatures, which were all part of the food chain and would turn his sterile waters into a fine, prolific brew of trout food.

Dipping from tanks mounted in the back of a pick-up truck, he poured in bucket after bucket of big-finned sculpins and slender spotted dace, minnows that would remain tiny and could be counted on to keep in balance without overpowering the food supply. They, in turn, would provide an excellent food source for larger fish. He watched with satisfaction as the tiny fry scurried for cover and vanished.

During the next weeks, the Major tramped up and down his waterway, planting insect larvae of dragon fly, caddis, and stonefly. And crustaceans such as daphne and amphipods such as fairy shrimp. He visited the Williamson, the Wood, the Sprague, the Malheur, Metolius, Powder, and the Burnt, wading with a net, lifting rocks, and scooping samples of stream life into ten gallon cream cans. Whatever his take, he rushed it back to the old Pittock place and planted it in his stream.

On his travels, the Major also did a good deal of serious shopping for brook trout stock. He drove from one private hatchery to another in Idaho, Montana, and Oregon looking for a trout farm free of disease, of superior reputation and stock.

In Idaho he found a fish farmer whose hatchery was located on a clear, dashing mountain brook, downstream from nobody, who had imported his breeders from a northern river that had consistently produced record brook trout.

"Brookies," said the farmer, "are both my passion and my hobby."

They also turned out to be his business. After hours of staring down into one holding pen after another, peering at thousands of darting trout, the Major made his selection, one lone female who was strong, active, wild, beautifully marked, and had outgrown her siblings by a third.

"You got quite an eye," the farmer said. "That's one I was going to save for breeding stock." He named an outrageous figure for the large trout, and probably wished he'd doubled it when the Major calmly took out his wallet and paid him cash.

Even in that mass of trout bodies, the young female

was so magnificent she was easy to locate. By using a system of screens, they were soon able to isolate the specimen in a small area, net her, and transfer her splendid body to a wooden box containing a large plastic bag of water.

The Major ballooned the bag out with a hose from a tank of pure oxygen, and once his cargo had been iced and covered with canvas, he jumped into his station wagon, waved, and drove off. He sped the six hundred odd miles home like a man with a death wish, hardly stopping for tea.

As he passed his house, he honked for Belle, gave her a perfunctory kiss on the cheek as she loaded up, and together they drove to the fields at the edge of the stream.

Carefully, hardly daring to look, he peeled back the canvas and exposed the large, deep trout swimming placidly in the container.

"There she is," the Major said proudly. "Isn't she a beauty?"

Belle stared down into the box. "One fish? That's all you brought home? One fish?"

The Major nodded. "Of course. I'm naming her 'The Virgin Queen'."

"One fish!" Belle said weakly.

"One fish," the Major said, his eyes gleaming. "Just think, Belle. The largest eastern brook trout ever caught on a fly was a fourteen and a half pounder. Alone in our river, with an unlimited food supply . . ."

"I see," Belle said, plunking herself down on a

rock. "The record is fourteen and a half pounds. And, one day, this one will weigh fifteen!"

"Twenty!" the Major corrected. "We'll leave her in the river for a while. What good is breaking a record only to have it broken a few seasons later?"

His eyes gleamed with a strange passion. "I deserve that record, Belle! Think of all those record fish I've turned loose. Why should posterity honor all those boobs who just happened to be lucky? After all, I'd only be claiming an honor that's rightfully mine. Remember that monster I caught in the Nippigon? She'd have gone seventeen, at least!"

Together, they lifted the plastic sphere out of the box and rolled it into a pool. The Major took out his stream thermometer and checked temperatures, first in the stream, then in the container. Slowly, he trickled water to the trout then checked again.

"What are you doing?" Belle asked.

"The inside temperature should match that of the stream. Otherwise the Queen might shock and die."

The fish swam about calmly, its gill covers working as it took in oxygen over its great pink gills.

"Fifty-five degrees outside," the Major said, taking the temperature again. "Fifty-five degrees inside. We're ready to turn her loose!"

He took a knife from his pocket, opened a blade, and slit the plastic. As the waters mingled, the big trout darted for freedom. One moment the hen was a large shadow in the gravelly shallows of the new river, the next she was gone.

12

"Why, it's Plummey, The Wild Boy of the Woodlands," said Mr. Goodrich, the storekeeper, as Plummey bounded up the front steps of the store. "And by that hankering look he's got in his eye, I know this poor old shopkeeper's going to come out a loser."

Plummey grinned. "You'll be a winner, this time, Mr. Goodrich. Not a thing on my mind but doing you a small favor. You know that old dusty box of bamboo stripping up in the storeroom that's been taking up space you could be using for saleable goods? Would you let me haul it away for you?"

"You mean that tube marked Horrocks Ibbotson, containing those delicate, antique, bamboo strips, which, shaved down to equilateral triangles, fitted together, glued and finished, would make a gleaming hexagon of a thousand-dollar fly rod?" Mr. Goodrich grinned.

Plummey's face fell. "Two Saturdays," he offered. "Not another kid in town as handy to have around as I am!"

"Museum pieces," Mr. Goodrich went on. "Should bring a small fortune from a collector. I should phone Major Quillaine."

"Three Saturdays, Mr. Goodrich. And gosh, that's during fishing season!"

"My heart bleeds," said the storekeeper. "Go on, Plummey. Take them. They're yours. Gratis. Free for nothing. And while you're up in the storeroom, take those old house cat hides you sold me once, claiming they were blue mink. The moths are at them."

"Gee, thanks, Mr. Goodrich!"

"One condition though," the storekeeper said. "The rod project has to be done right. No sense ruining good wood. Old Sluter, the blind man, lives in a cabin out at the end of Front Street; they tell me he was quite a rod-maker once. You stop by there and ask him how. There's an art to it or I would have made those sticks up for myself long ago."

Plummey bounded up the stairs to the storeroom, came down with the long, dusty container, then left abruptly as though fearful that Mr. Goodrich would change his mind. "Thanks again, Mr. Goodrich," he called back over his shoulder. "I'll be back to get the skins when I've got more time."

He knew where Mr. Sluter's cabin was. A log house with a blue shake roof. He even knew Mr. Sluter, sort of. Helped the old man across an intersection just the other day; just took his arm without saying anything. Never knew what to talk to a blind man about. What if you said something to hurt his feelings. Like,

"Sure is a beautiful sunset isn't it?" Easier not to start a conversation at all.

Plummey knocked at the cabin door and, for a moment, thought there was no one home. Then he heard bedsprings creak, a groaning complaint common to old age, the shuffling of carpet slippers on linoleum, then the *tap, tap tap*ping of the blind man's white cane.

"Who is it?" Mr. Sluter called. "Who's out there? What do you want?"

"It's just me, Mr. Sluter. Plummey Pittock. I live over by the river. Mr. Goodrich over at the store said you were an expert once at making bamboo fly rods. He gave me the makings and said I should ask you how."

A bolt clicked, and the door opened. "Come in! Come in!" the old man said. " 'An expert once,' did he say? Well, next time you see that Goodrich, you tell him I'm still an expert! Being blind, that's an asset. Got eyes in my fingertips now. Just like micrometers they are."

He groped for Plummey's elbow and led him across the threshold, steering him toward a straight-backed chair. "Sit down! Sit down!" He himself shuffled toward a big red leather rocking chair. Though white haired and stooped in the shoulders, the man's skin was as pink and smooth as a baby's, and his hands looked surprisingly supple and strong. He found his great chair and sat down.

"Don't fish much anymore though. Once in a while Major Quillaine takes me down to the river and lets me cast. You talk fly fishing do you? Ought to get together with the Major. Gets lonesome, sometimes, the Major does. Says there's nobody around this town but me talks fish talk."

"I've brought the bamboo," Plummey said, still ill at ease. He took the bundle of dry sticks from the carton and laid it in the old man's hand, then sat and watched as Mr. Sluter ran his fingers up and down the strips, flexing each one separately.

Plummey came right to the point. "Mr. Sluter, I don't have money, but maybe I could get in your fire-wood. I notice you have a wood stove."

"How come you want a bamboo rod, boy?" he asked. "Most young folks now are crazy for fiberglass, graphite, or even boron."

"It's Major Quillaine," Plummey replied. "I was watching him cast. It was so beautiful I made up my mind some day I'd learn to cast like that. Or even better. And the Major—he uses bamboo."

"Better than the Major!" The old rod maker chuckled. "Well, young man, you'd better start practicing!"

"Bamboo rods cost lots of money," Plummey said, "and I realized if ever I was going to own one, I'd have to get the material and make it myself."

"Better than the Major!" Mr. Sluter smiled. He picked up the bamboo again, felt of it, sniffed it, then flexed it carefully, inch by inch. He turned his sightless eyes toward Plummey thoughtfully. "Well, lad, let me tell you something. You'll not out-cast the Major with a rod built of this. Don't misunderstand me. It's good wood all right, but not great. The Major, he's got a Pinky Gillum, a Jim Payne, or an Everett Garrison for every day of the week. Plus a super one-piece Orvis and a Winston. I'll help you make your first rod out of this, but it'll be just for practice. When the time comes, we can talk about better things."

He rose from his chair and felt along the wall until he came to an oak cabinet, opened it, and took out a gleaming fly rod, its varnish dark with age. "Here," he said. "Take a look at this, and you'll know what a good rod should feel like. Made it myself, of course."

"Is this your last rod?" Plummey asked.

"Nope," Mr. Sluter replied. "God willing, I haven't made my last one. I made this one when I was a boy your age. My father taught me. He was a stickler for detail; I came near hating him over this rod, just as one day you may come to hate me. But if you're game to try, son, why I may just make a great fly rod man out of you."

Plummey watched as the old man greased the ferrule with a film of oil from the side of his nose, put it together and handed it to him. He held the rod stiffly, not quite knowing what he was expected to do; it was the first bamboo rod he'd ever held. The guides were bound with red and purple silk and shone like burnished silver. It was more than just a rod; it was a gleaming masterpiece!

He put it back into Mr. Sluter's hand, as though not wanting the responsibility for holding it, and took up his bundle of bamboo. He felt depressed; how could he ever pare those clumsy sticks down into equilateral triangles, perfectly matched in size and taper?

The blind man seemed to sense his mood and to understand his discouragement. "I know how you feel." He smiled. "When I was a lad and took up that first bundle of sticks, I thought that there was no chance in the world my clumsy paws could ever make them into something. One step at a time, I kept at it. Well, you can see the results."

The old man put the rod carefully back into the glass case, then moved to his bed and eased along it. Midway, he knelt down, and Plummey thought for a moment he was going to say his prayers. Instead, the old craftsman groped beneath, dragged out a dusty box, pulled himself to his feet, and carried it to his workbench.

"Now, lad," he said, as he opened it up. "These are the tools of the trade, and by the time you get that rod made, you're going to be good at using every one of them."

13

Most folks have everything to give the old and disabled except the thing they often need most. Time. The working relationship that developed between Plummey and the blind rodmaker was good for them both. The boy was not one who would accept Mr. Sluter's services for nothing. Soon Mr. Sluter had the biggest pile of dry split juniper firewood in town. Since Plummey had no driver's license, he prevailed upon his mother to haul it in the family pickup truck. Piled against the cabin wall in meticulous stacks, it gave the little house an appearance of being far bigger than it really was. He also shopped for groceries, picked up mail, ran errands, and on Mr. Sluter's rare walks down along Main Street, became his seeing eye dog.

Plummey's big hands were deceptive. He had a way with a knife, knew how to sharpen tools, and showed a rare coordination between hand and eye. These attributes, coupled with a desire to do things right and master a craft, made Mr. Sluter pleased, even excited over his progress.

In his back shed, the old man had an oven for hardening the bamboo, a pressure tank to force resins into the pores to waterproof the rod, and a planing form or jig, a long piece of steel with tapered grooves into which each strip would be placed for shaping.

Plummey followed instructions and smoothed down the outer nodes on each of the strips, being careful not to harm the outer enamel on the back of the strip. When he had finished, Mr. Sluter put on heavy gloves, baked the strips in the oven, straightened the wood over the flame of a torch, then impregnated them with resin. He then placed the sticks enameled side down into the tapered grooves and showed Plummey how to plane the sides into a tapered isosceles triangle.

Every few minutes, the old man would rub his fingers over the wood and read his progress.

"No," he might say. "Here you are going too deep. Gently! Gently! Take your time. You can always take more off, but never, never can you put some back. It's slow work, Plummey. Now you know why bamboo rods cost so much money. Nobody wants to put in the time any more. For every ten cents of material, it takes a hundred dollars of finesse and patience."

Even after the piece appeared to Plummey to be finished, Mr. Sluter ran his fingers across it and shook his head. "Right here! Take a shard of broken glass and scrape off the tiniest whisper. Use the micrometer when the fingers tell you nothing."

When, at last, he could find no more fault, he smiled and patted Plummey's shoulder. "Now," he said, "you've done one. Do five more perfectly matched."

The project took longer than Plummey had planned. On one of his rare visits to his tree house, he found that a big garden spider had taken over and spun a skein of webs. At the moment Plummey peered up through the trapdoor, the spider was in the process of devouring a damsel fly. Since he was due over at Mr. Sluter's, he left the spider in possession of the little house.

He hoped no one would waylay him as he biked into town. Now that folks knew where to find him, they gave him plenty of odd jobs to do. Since money was tight around home, Plummey felt obligated to take whatever job was offered. It seemed as though the jobs went painfully slow, while time at Mr. Sluter's whisked past all too quickly.

Here I am, Plummey thought to himself, one day, on my way to becoming a maker of fine rods, and I'm cleaning out Old Lady Nelson's chicken house! Nonetheless, the three silver dollars she found for him when the chicken house was spotless helped soothe his pride a good bit.

That night he gave his mother a big hug as she labored over the hot wood stove and danced the silver coins. "How do you like those?" he teased. "The first ever from my new profession."

"Making rods?" she asked surprised.

"No, cleaning chicken houses. Old Lady Nelson thought I had a nice touch with a manure fork and a wheelbarrow. She's going to recommend me to her friends."

"Well, I'm glad she didn't pay you in eggs the way she did last time. Our own chickens keep us more than supplied." She glanced up from her cooking just in time to catch Plummey with his hand in the cookie jar.

"Tell me," she asked, ignoring the theft. "How is the rod making coming along?"

"Pretty well," he answered. "Boy, does that old man ever know his stuff. It takes time, but when I get done, I'll have something far better than just a beautiful fly rod. I'll have learned a skill, and that's the best thing of all." He munched the last of a chocolate chip cookie, then rattled the tops of the pans, sniffing out the supper. "And when I've got that rod, I'm going to become the best fly-fisherman in the whole world. Better even than Major Quillaine. Just you wait and see!"

Mrs. Pittock smiled and bent to open the oven, bringing out a large platter on which she had baked a trout.

"Hey," Plummey said. "I don't remember catching that one."

"You didn't. Your old mother did. Your poor old steel fishing pole looked so lonesome over there in the corner, and while I was gardening, I found a big fat night crawler and—"

Plummey looked shocked. "You didn't," he said. "Gosh, I don't know how to take that, Mom. A bait fisherman in the family. Wow!"

He put his arm around his mother and gave her a

big hug. She was full of surprises, that woman. He resolved that someday soon he was going to build a fly rod just for her.

The next morning, he rose early and did his chores. Today was a big day for him; Mr. Sluter had finally passed on his strips and promised to show him how to cement them all together.

Once the glue had been applied to the strips, with the nodes or weak spots staggered as planned, his instructor ran the bundle through a pressure gluing machine, which applied heavy pressure to the bundle while it wound it in two directions with heavy twine.

When the glue had set and the twine was removed, the old man put on his gloves again and straightened the bends and twists in the rod over a flame, holding the rod straight until it cooled. After the excess cement had been sanded off, Mr. Sluter took the slender piece in his hand.

"Now," he said. "We may have built ourselves a Stradivarius, but even the finest violin must be tuned." He laid the tip on the flat table and rolled it with his fingertips. "There! You see the little hop? It should roll smoothly like an egg."

He felt the wood with his fingers. "Yes, of course! Now I feel it. Just a tiny wipe or two of emery cloth. One here. One there."

He rotated the piece once more. "Better now, but still a little hop. Another wipe, this time with steel wool. See there? Smooth as custard!"

The butt of the rod seemed far easier than the tip. Once the pieces had been planed in the jig, they seemed to fall together.

"Look at that, Mr. Sluter!" Plummey said one day, as the rod, complete with ferrules, handle, reel seat, guides, and a fresh coat of varnish, was hung to dry from a wire to the ridgepole. He flushed suddenly, realizing that Mr. Sluter couldn't see. The way the old man could do things, it was easy to forget.

Mr. Sluter only laughed. "Oh, I'll look at it soon enough, Plummey, my boy. Only I'll wait until the varnish has dried; then it will be those special little eyes in my fingertips I'll use."

He got up from his workbench. "You've made your first rod and done a pretty fair job. I've got a graduation present for you." He felt his way along the wall to an old oak cabinet. Rummaging through drawers, he touched the contents of each as though visiting friends.

"Here," he said, pulling out a little reel wound with line. "Here's a little Hardy reel and a line that should balance out just right on the new rod. I don't want any money for it, and I'm scared to death you're going to bring me more wood. Why I've got enough stacked outside my house to last my poor little stove for years. Take it, Plummey, and put it to good use. From one fisherman to another."

"Gosh!" Plummey stammered. "Gosh, Mr. Sluter. Thanks! Could we try it out? I mean could we take the rod and reel down to the river soon?"

"River!" Mr. Sluter snorted. "You *are* in a hurry. You're not ready for the river yet."

He took a tapered leader from a cellophane wrapper, then felt about and picked a fly from a fly box. "Now," he said, taking a coffee cup from the sink. "Take my rod, while yours is drying, and let's go out on the back lawn. That's where you'll do your casting for a while. That is, if you want me to make a flycaster out of you, too."

"Lawn" was not the word for it. It hadn't been watered for years and was nothing but a flat, dry, bare piece of ground. Already a few tiny junipers were taking command. But it had once been loved. Plummey could see traces of what had once been flower gardens along the border, but they had gone along with Mr. Sluter's sight.

The old man installed the reel and worked the tip of the line through the guides. That done, he tied on a tapered leader, and even threaded the tip of the leader through the eye of the tiny fly. The boy marveled at his dexterity.

"There," Mr. Sluter said with satisfaction. "Now, we'll make her dance!" He handed Plummey the cup. "Put it out there about twenty feet for starters," he directed. "Cast your line out forward, stop it about three feet in the air, and let it float down into the cup."

He handed the rod to Plummey and stepped back out of the way. He tried his best to cast, but behind him the line cracked like a whip, and the fly hit him on the back of the neck. Again and again he tried.

"Give me the rod," Mr. Sluter said. "Here! Like

70

this." With a flick of the rod tip, he rolled the line into the air, sent it flying far out behind him, then smoothly forward. "See that?" he asked. "Let the rod do the work." He handed the tackle back to Plummey.

The boy felt embarrassed, but his jaw set in determination to succeed.

"Gently now," the old man said. "Relax. Pause on the back cast to let the line straighten out behind you, then shoot it forward. Pretend you're throwing a dart. Just the tiniest flick of the wrist!"

The line sailed out smoothly enough, but on the back cast the fly dropped near the ground and snagged a young juniper. Patiently, Plummey tried again. This time he slapped the fly out on the ground before him. A slow anger began to burn within him. He felt like a fool. Mr. Sluter must be laughing at him.

"You're thinking about water," the man said. "Forget it. There's no water and no fish. Stop that fly in the air and let it float down into the cup."

Plummey tried, but the fly missed the cup by six feet. Again he sent the fly on its tour. Again he let the fly float downward, barely missing the white mug. "Better!" he cried out.

"Send it back, flying out behind you, hold it, now forward," instructed Mr. Sluter. "That fly's a hummer. I tied it on purpose so I could tell its whereabouts just by listening. A little more time, please, on the back cast."

Back and forth, the fly hummed.

"Better," the blind man said. "And now the cup!"

The fly stopped in mid-flight and floated down gently like the breast feather of a duck. To Plummey's amazement, it landed right in the cup.

"There!" he cried out excitedly. "I made the cup. Can I try her on the river now, Mr. Sluter? Please?"

"The river!" Mr. Sluter snorted. "Always it's the river! No, my boy, the river would only spoil you at this point. You're going to work right here on dry land until your casting is part of you, so that you can make that fly dance the way a mountain lion controls the black tip on the end of his tail. You told me you wanted to be a flycaster. Well, young Plummey Pittock, I'm going to make you one!"

14

THE MAJOR was having a good day. He worked his way downstream across his land, fishing in turn pools from the Battenkill, Silver Creek, and the Laughing Whitefish. Often he would cease his casting to peer into the water, noting how well the plant and animal life were taking over the new system.

He turned over a waterlily pad and found jellylike egg masses, lifted a piece of driftwood and peered back at hundreds of startled fairy shrimp and water fleas. Dragonflies patrolled the pools, cruising for other insects to devour. Blue damselflies clustered on the bur reed.

Over the banks, the wild rice bent, nodded, and waved in the wind, heads already heavy with shaggy-coated kernels. In the cool of the cottonwoods and aspens, a light breeze turned tiny fanlike leaves on their petioles; and the columbines Belle had transplanted waved their tiny birdlike blossoms, as though they had been there always.

The Major was not worried about catching the Virgin Queen. He knew exactly where she had taken up residence. She had had her choice of any pool in the stream, but had chosen a churn of heavily aerated water below the horseshoe falls, lying deep during the day, moving out into the riffles during evening hatches. Bloated with food, when she leaped she had the outline of a pumpkin seed.

For weeks after he had released her, the Major had seen no sign. Then, one evening, he heard the rattle of a kingfisher and knew that the bird had seen the shadow of a working fish. A week later he watched an osprey, flying leisurely upstream, stop to circle, hover over the horseshoe rock, then go on its way as if deciding that the fish it saw was too big to tackle. That night as the Major sat at the pool waiting, listening, he heard a *kerchunk*, the unmistakable sound of a feeding fish. In the half darkness, he saw ripples fading away.

Often, in the evening, the Major and Belle would stroll upstream from their house to the pool to sit out the twilight, feel the cool kiss of spray on their cheeks, and, watching the progression of hatches, listen for the faint plash of their one trout. The Major suddenly found himself fearing Death, for he could not imagine anything in the afterlife that could remotely approach this.

He was so content, he had almost forgotten about Plummey Pittock and his tree house. He'd heard that the boy was spending most of his time in town, hanging around old Sluter, for what reason he could not guess. Used to be a master fly-fisherman, that old man. He couldn't conceive that Sluter and that damned poacher would have anything to talk about.

Ruefully one evening, as the damp of his river rose about him, he rolled his shoulder, feeling a dull pain. Sometimes now it woke him in the night, and it was hours before he could sleep again. Now he tied on a Quillaine's quill. He liked the fly. Enough hackle to make it float on the summer air like thistledown, yet just the proper weight for control. On the water it rode high, daring the surface tension, like an insect poised for take-off. Teasing a trout to hurry.

Now as though to prove to himself that he was still a master, he rolled the quill out over the Queen's pool and made it hover where he thought she lay. In his intense concentration he forgot his shoulder. Again and again he danced the fly across the water, not daring to let it land lest the big trout rise to it. Perfection! He remembered an exhibition in Kansas City, when he was, quite possibly, at the height of his powers. He had executed a series so powerful yet so controlled that the crowd around the casting pool had gasped and stood in shattered silence before someone dared applaud.

The wind seemed to hush now in deference to his art. Inspired by the beauty of the river he had created, he cast as he had not done in years. Long, slow rolls of incredible distance, dominating the pool, perfect in accuracy and control. He went through a whole cadenza of stunts, acrobatic casts one never did on a stream but were more the province of the exhibition artist.

He had a feeling that someone watched him from

afar. The poacher, maybe, from his tree house. Well, let him stare. All this would be wasted on the boy and way beyond anything he could comprehend.

Then, because he had always believed that the function of a fly-cast was to impress fish, not people, he executed a brilliant series of dances with his quill to imitate the vertical rhapsody of the mayfly. Had there been a lesser fish in the pool than the Virgin Queen, he knew it would have been compelled to leap for his fly.

His arm ached miserably, but he went on, ceasing only when Belle came striding across the meadows with a basket of fried chicken and a bottle of white wine for their supper.

"Major," she said, her eyes shining with pleasure. "You do cast up a storm!"

She would have set the picnic by the great rock, but the Major stopped her and led her to the dell she had planted so prettily with columbine. To the Major, there was something sacred about a trout stream that made it not for picnicking.

As twilight fell and a big moon came up over the rimrocks, they returned to the pool and sat quietly, arm in arm, watching the water. The chill of autumn sank into the hollows along the river, and the two leaned together for warmth. A family of mink, nose to tail, looking like a long piece of wet black rope, moved down the shallows along the far shore, then split up to search for crayfish among the cobbles. Both the pool and the riffle, however, seemed deserted.

"She's there somewhere," the Major whispered, as though to quash an unexpressed dread. His fly, strangely enough, hadn't managed even to tease her into a boil. Maybe she had moved on to another pool. Or maybe that damned poacher . . .

There was a patter of tiny dace in the shallows as they stood on their tails trying to flee some foe. The water dimpled, and the head of a water snake surfaced, a three-inch dace wriggling in its jaws. The snake moved easily across the rippling gold of the moon path and disappeared into the forest of wild rice along the shore. They could hear the sound of distant waterfalls, now near, now far as the wind changed directions in the night.

"Let's go," Belle said. "It's getting chilly."

"Wait," the Major said. "Five more minutes. There are still some big dusky millers about. All it takes is for one to flutter close to that riffle."

For a time no millers moved. Then there was a fluttering in the grass across the stream, and a big gray moth went winging out over the dance of moonlight on the riffle. *Kerchunk!* The Virgin Queen, gleaming with ghostly luminescence, leaped high and took the foolish insect in a gulp, then rolled back, splashing water on the bank. The riffle healed itself, the bubbles sailed off around the bend, and the pool was silent once more as though the action had never been.

15

PLUMMEY LAY in his bedroll in the tree house, so excited he could hardly wait for morning. Such casts as he had seen the evening before! He had hardly dreamed them possible. Far from discouraging him, he had taken each brilliant series as a new goal to be mastered. Watching from high above, he had let his body become an extension of the Major's. From that vantage point he had seen tricks that might not have been discernable to a watcher at ground level. That slight, ever so subtle, flick of the wrist that cast a rolling loop into the line and made the fly dance over the water. Timing! And coordination of wrist with line. The coach had been after him to go out for football, but in the light of what he had seen the Major do, that stuff seemed pure silliness.

Plummey stretched out his toes lazily and pushed against the bottom of his bedroll, looking out past the yellow leaves of the cottonwood at the clouds draped like gray laundry on the long ridgepole of the Cascades to the west. Clouds like that spelled snow and would leave a white shroud over the high country. School would start next week. There was going to be a big get-acquainted dance in the gym, Saturday night.

He didn't guess he'd even go. Probably go over to Mr. Sluter's instead. That tall blonde girl, Betty Carlson, would be at the dance looking for him. A couple of times last spring, when he'd been dressed up in his Sunday best for church, he'd managed to walk past her place, looking straight ahead though, as if he were on his way somewhere.

If she'd come out of her house, he wouldn't have known what to talk to her about. It would be worse asking her to dance. I mean you had to say something! Maybe he could ask her if she was into fly-fishing. Ha! Ha!

He wondered how the Major had found a girl like Mrs. Quillaine? He hoped he could find one like that someday. Someone to share things with. Someone who was kind of into Nature the way he was, who wouldn't scream if she saw a harmless old water snake and might even think being up here in the tree house was super cool.

The frost was still on the rocks in Mr. Sluter's back yard when Plummey arrived to practice. He was glad school hadn't started yet; he could cast until his arm got sore. It seemed to him the old man would never get out of bed and come out to see what he was doing.

He had the opening roll of the cast down perfect,

and he was working on the twist, sending the fly dancing. Now he understood why Mr. Sluter insisted he
learn on dry land. One's concentration had to be total.
No time to worry about water and fish. Just the rod,
line, leader, fly, and the wrist. He had it! The fly was
dancing!

"What on earth?" Mr. Sluter said, coming out on
his back stoop. "Where did you learn that? Only the
Major does those tricks. I can hear that fly dancing!"
He stood for a few minutes, listening critically to the
rhythms, but could find no fault.

"Listen to this!" Plummey said, making the fly skip
enticingly across the ground like a mayfly emerging on
first flight from a wave. "Am I ready for the river yet,
Mr. Sluter?"

So intent was he on the answer, that he lost his
concentration and the fly line wound miserably around
his neck.

The old man heard the sounds and smiled. "Not
yet," he said. "But you're getting the hang of it. It's
like a golf swing. You do it and do it until it becomes
part of you, and then you can concentrate on the rest
of the game."

The blind man moved slowly from his door, groped
for a bench and sat down, then went on. "When the
Major walks down the street and casts an imaginary line
to his friends, you think that's just an amusing mannerism; but actually, I suppose, he's keeping his hand in.
Like a boxer shadow boxing when he jogs, stopping now
and then to throw a few punches in the air. A boxer can

get away with it, and folks understand. Boxing is athletics. But for a fly-fisherman to cast when there isn't a river in sight, that's another matter."

He smiled patiently at Plummey. "Next spring," he said, "we'll go down to the river together. Until then, I want you to cast and cast and cast."

That afternoon, Plummey finished up some odd jobs around town and dropped by the bank to deposit the money he had collected to his mom's account. He sighed as the envelope disappeared into the slot. He had been tempted to keep a little out, just to have some in his pocket. "A little jingling money," Mr. Sluter would have called it. But there was nothing he really needed.

Across the street, he saw Mr. Goodrich strolling past, slightly tilted forward by his big belly, slapping the ground firmly with his high shoes at each step, as though killing snakes. Imitating the Major, Plummey cast an imaginary fly across the street, and Mr. Goodrich stared at him for a moment, putting together the joke, then laughed aloud and cast one back. He felt somehow that in stealing the Major's pet mannerism, it made the man seem less formidable.

Mr. Sluter was asleep in his chair when he came in. He put some chicken soup on for the old man's supper and made himself a peanut butter sandwich. As the tea water began to sing in the kettle, Mr. Sluter awoke with a start. "Oh, it's you! The world's greatest flycaster."

"Not yet." Plummey grinned. "But some day."

The old man sat for some minutes considering something, then seemed to make a weighty decision. He took his cane and pointed up into the rafters. "Look up there and tell me what you find."

Plummey did what he was told. He stood on the workbench and peered into the gloom.

"Well, what's up there?"

"Nothing but dust. Wait. A long piece of bamboo."

"Well, boy, notice anything about it?"

"It's split in two sections lengthwise," Plummey replied.

"What else? What else?"

"It's a lot further between nodes than regular bamboo."

"Exactly, exactly! It's a rare piece of Tsinglee cane from China, and a freak of nature. Never saw one as good. You might build a rod out of it that could out-perform any in the land."

"And could I outperform the Major?"

Mr. Sluter smiled. "Boy, you could own the finest rod in the world and not out-cast the Major. Not without years of practice, dedication, know-how, and natural talent. And mix in Lady Luck."

Plummey brought down the long cane. The old man took it from his hands and wiped it with a towel. Plummey could tell it meant a lot to him.

"It's been seasoning for years," Mr. Sluter said. "It was split once to keep it from checking. Time now you cut it into six pieces to make a rod of it. You ready, lad?"

"I'm scared," Plummey said. "I keep thinking of what-ifs. Like, what if it doesn't split straight? What if there's a tiny check, or a wormhole we can't see? And what if I make a slip with the chisel or plane?"

"How about what if the two of us make the greatest rod that was ever built? I already have a name for it. 'Excalibur,' after King Arthur's sword!"

Patiently, the old rod-maker showed Plummey how to insert a small froe, a handle with a sharp, wedgelike blade jutting off at a right angle. "Perfect?" he asked Plummey.

"Looks straight," Plummey said.

Calmly, the blind man tapped the froe with a mallet to start the split, then moved the blade through the wood until the strip fell off. "There's the first," he said.

"Now five more," Plummey said.

The wood was as perfect as it looked. Six long strips lay before them on the workbench, each as wondrous as another.

"Towel, please," Mr. Sluter said. He had seemed so calm, but now that it was over, his forehead was covered with perspiration. "Enough for one day! A piece like this we don't want to hurry."

Carefully, Plummey laid the strips back up in the rafters where they wouldn't be broken. To relax, he took his new rod down from the ceiling, added reel, line, leader, and fly and went out back to try it out.

He wet his finger and held it up. A light breeze off the desert sage. Not much to compensate for. He rolled the line into the air. Back and forth. Back and forth. The rod began to do the work and felt good. He felt a shiver of excitement run through his body. His very own rod; his first bamboo!

"Excellent!" Mr. Sluter said from nearby. "Now let her float. Carefully! Keep control! Superb! Right in the cup!"

"You're not blind at all," Plummey said. "It did go in. How could you tell?"

"Body language." Mr. Sluter smiled. "I could hear your heart pound. Now. Again. A little more slack with the left hand and a little less tense. You're improving fast. I can tell from the sound. Ah, what music the line makes!"

Plummey cast until his arm was so weary he could hardly hold it up. It was as though the rod were an extension of his body, and the line a nerve that carried orders from his brain right out to the fly. What was it Mr. Sluter had said? "The way a mountain lion controls the tip of its long tail?"

Often now the fly floated down into the cup. So the old man made him back up to increase his range. "Pretty soon." The old man grinned. "You're going to have to start using a shot glass instead of that big coffee mug."

16

PLUMMEY WAS OFF working about town the afternoon Major Quillaine knocked on the door of Mr. Sluter's log house.

"Come in, Major," the old man called, recognizing the heavy, rhythmic knock.

Mr. Sluter sat in the one good piece of furniture left from better times, a red Morocco leather rocking chair stuffed with horsehair, generously dimpled with buttons, and fluted with pleats. It rode on two beautifully ornate, winged, mahogany dragons. There wasn't a week when Mr. Sluter didn't saddle soap the leather or polish the rockers with oil.

You could read the mood the old man was in by whether or not he set the wedges under the rockers. Happy and content, he rocked up a storm; anxious or upset, he set wedges under the rockers and sat primly upright.

His new friendship with Plummey had given him

much to look forward to, and now he sat with wedges out, rocking contentedly as he played his radio and sucked on an old S-shanked pipe, enjoying the heat from the bowl of his gnarled old fingers.

The Major cast him a fly then realized it was a wasted effort. "It's the old rod-maker himself," the Major said cheerfully.

"Don't know who else it would be," Mr. Sluter replied. He felt a certain tension in the air. The Major wanted something, and he wished he would get on with it. "What can I do for you, Major?" he asked.

"Just passing by and thought I'd look in on you," the Major replied. "Ran water down through my stream system late in the spring. You'd be surprised at what I've built. It's like a living museum display of some of the greatest trout pools in America. Should take you down to see it some day."

"I'd like that," Mr. Sluter replied. "The seeing part especially."

"Oh," the Major said.

Mr. Sluter got up, walked around to the back of his chair, kicked in the wedges, then returned and sat down again. He wished that Plummey would come back from whatever it was he was doing, so that they could do some more work on the rod.

Any other time but this he would have welcomed company. The Major was about to launch another fishing episode; he could feel it coming. A few diversions, and he would be into it.

"I've been doing some casting on the new stream," the Major said. "It's very satisfying. Just being able to cast and not have to worry about fishing. In one day on my own place, I can fish pools from the major rivers in North America. Think of it! Got a stretch there you'd swear was the Green. You ever try nymphing the Green?"

"Never fished the Green," Mr. Sluter said. "I expect some of my rods went there, but never me."

"Well, it's quite a river," the Major said. "I remember the first time I fished it back in the 'fifties. Fellow named Bob Derleth took me in. Helluva nymph man. Gone now. Shot at a cat in a tree with a bow and got hit with his own arrow. I was sitting in a bar nursing a very inadequate martini, when he came up to me and said, 'I see you're a fly-fisherman by the looks of your clothes.' I was still wearing my ultra-light chest waders and had a hat full of flies. He didn't have to be psychic to figure that out."

Mr. Sluter lit his pipe and leaned back. Maybe he could doze off without the Major knowing.

"Dress like that, you end up meeting local fishermen," the Major went on, "and you can pick their brains as to what hatches to expect. Well, to make a long story short, he offered to take me over on the Green the very next day.

"Well, we'd fished for some time without much action on the flies he'd recommended, when I took down a little deer hair floater I'd tied on a three X fine, fifteen hook, and put it on. 'What's that pool up ahead?' I asked my guide.

" 'Good lookin' pool, but it never yields many trout,' he said.

"Might there be a lunker hiding under yon cutbank?" I asked.

" 'I doubt it,' he answered, putting on down stream.

"Well, imagine his astonishment when I let that little deer hair bug carom off a pine log and float down past that cutbank. Why the largest trout I'd taken that month, sucked in my fly, and the fight was on. Eighteen and a quarter pounds! Can you believe it?"

Mr. Sluter could and did. No one ever doubted the Major. He was that good. He closed his eyes and remembered an episode from his own past when he was fishing an unnamed stream. With worms, probably. Likely he'd never seen a fly rod in those days of the Depression. A pretty girl, tall and slender as a willow, was having a picnic with her family and came strolling over to watch him fish; she'd stayed on for the next thirty-two years. If he caught any fish that day it wasn't important.

He wanted to lie back in his chair and doze until Plummey came back. Quite a boy, that one. Good hands and determination. If he didn't end up out-fishing the Major some day, he'd at least give him a helluva run.

"I was using my four and a quarter ounce Pinky Gillum rod," the Major went on, "and it was a test."

He cleared his throat. "Speaking of rods," he said,

getting around to the reason for his visit. "You once showed me an interesting culm of Tsinglee you had seasoning in your rafters. Thought if you'd sell it to me, I'd take it down to Klamath with me next time I have a go at the Williamson. There's a young rod-maker just set up shop down there, and I like his work. Might just have him make me a rod out of your wood."

Mr. Sluter sat with his eyes closed as though he hadn't heard. "So that's it," he thought. "All these years he's been so pleasant. He wants that culm. Thinks I can't make rods any more just because I can't see. Well, I can still build a mean rod and I can teach. I'll work on that Plummey so that some day he does out-cast and out-fish the Major."

"About the wood, Sluter. How much do you want for it? I don't have my checkbook with me today, but I can send the wife by."

"The wood?" Mr. Sluter said as though trying to place it. "Oh, that. Well, it's promised." He couldn't resist turning the screw.

"Promised?" the Major said in surprise. "I don't understand. I've talked about that piece for years."

"Promised," said Mr. Sluter. "I've got a friend who is one of the great flycasters of all time. Asked me to make a one-piece rod of that culm for him. Think of it, Major. Why that freak piece of Tsinglee cane will make a rod to beat any in the land."

"I'll give you double what he offered," the Major said in anguish. "Triple!"

"Major, you wouldn't be able to give me triple what my friend paid. You see, I gave it to him as a gift!"

The Major hadn't been gone half an hour when Plummey came in the door.

"Oh," Mr. Sluter said. "It's you. The former champion was just here before you. Wanted to buy that culm of cane."

"What river did he fish today?" Plummey asked.

"This time it was the Green."

"Oh that," Plummey said, moving into the Major's character. "I remember the first time I fished it, back in the 'fifties. Fellow named Derleth took me in. Helluva nymph man. Was sitting in a bar nursing a martini when he came up to me and said, 'I see you're a fly fisherman from the looks of your clothes—' "

"You've got it!" Mr. Sluter chuckled.

"Sat behind him the other night at the movie, *On Golden Pond*. Paid good money to take my mom and all we got to hear was the Major."

Plummey looked suddenly serious. "When I get to be a great fly-fisherman like the Major, I hope I don't become a bore."

"Maybe you won't," Mr. Sluter said. "But then again, maybe you will. Perhaps it goes with the turf."

17

THE WINTER was unusually cold. It pleased the Major that whereas many of the areas of the Deschutes suffered long periods of winter dormancy where no insect hatched and no fish rose, in his river system the Virgin Queen remained active, boiling after midges along sheltered bends where the sun managed to warm the brown, exposed soils along the banks. Now and again, in the faint winter sunshine, he caught a flash of silver set with garnet, as she rolled playfully in a swirl.

If, surrounded by thousands of other fish in the hatchery, the Virgin Queen had out-hustled her class-mates for food, now, with no competition, she might have become lazy. Instead, she still quested eagerly, as though each insect hatch were the last. Moving rest-lessly, where another fish might have lain quiet, she bumped stones with her nose, turning up crayfish, fairy shrimp, and caddis larvae.

Even during cold winter nights, when the moon

hung over the snowscape like a frozen honeydew melon, and it was all the Major could do to huddle in his Eddie Bauer goosedown, steelhead outfit, he sometimes caught a boil and churn of the murky waters as she fed. And sometimes, as he ceased to believe that she existed and decided to seek the comfort of home, fire, and wife, the trout leaped in a great rainbow arc over the pool, drenching him with icy spray as his heart pounded with excitement. Never had he known a fish to grow so fast. Already she was in the record class.

Once, as he walked his river after a fresh snow, he found human footprints that belonged neither to him nor to Belle, and he bristled with anger, guessing that the Pittock boy had been snooping. If that damned poacher knew about the Queen, he'd stop at nothing to catch her. He followed the tracks, expecting to come across the boy in every new vista, but they crossed a fallen log well above the huge trout's haunts, circled through the brush along the Deschutes, then cut back across the bottom and up over the rimrock to the Upper Pittock.

In his daydreams, the Major set all sorts of traps for the boy. Tiger pits camouflaged with brush and lined with rows of sharpened stakes; deadfalls of logs set to crush the enemy as he ignored the boundaries of the Major's property. Based on footprints alone, he thought he could have the law on the boy for trespassing; but such laws were only as effective as the local justice of the peace found them important. Young Pittock would at best get a slap on the wrist, nothing more, and go on poaching as had his father and his grandfather before him.

He checked out the cottonwood tree, but found no tracks to indicate that the boy had been using his tree house, and felt relieved. With the leaves gone, the shack high in the tree looked cold and forbidding. He hoped fervently that a winter storm would swoop down off the Cascades to take the old tree down, smashing the tree house to smithereens.

The Major heard a tapping from above and stiffened, but it was only a wintering flicker drumming a tattoo on the boards. It flew off toward the cottonwood groves along the river, golden feathers flashing, rising and falling with each burst of wingbeats until it was lost from view.

The man thought of taking a wrecking bar to the platform, sending the tree house crashing downward as though a winter storm had done it. Interests of boys that age had a way of changing anyway. Girls took over. And sports. Once the vantage point high in the old tree were destroyed, the boy might be too lazy to build it again; and, if the platform in the tree were gone, the Virgin Queen would have a far better chance of remaining undetected.

But whatever thoughts he had of wrecking the tree house were stayed by an inner dread of what would happen if he were caught in the act and the newspapers picked it up. He could see the headlines. "Famous Flycaster Wrecks Boy's Treehouse!" Who but Belle would understand his love of the Virgin Queen, and the intensity of his dream?

Actually, the Major was to be given a few month's peace, for Plummey was busy elsewhere. Mr. Sluter had encouraged Plummey to go out for basketball.

"Good for the hands, my boy. Good for the hands."

The blind man liked nothing better than to attend the games, and it became a ritual for Plummey to deposit him in the bleachers above the local cheering section with a large bag of popcorn and take him home after the game. Mr. Sluter missed very little. He was adept at reading sounds, knew from the roar of the crowd just which team had the ball, from the pound and squeak of rubber on hardwood sensed just where the action was taking place. From the silence of those about him, he knew just when a free throw was in the offing, and from cheers or jeers whether or not it was successful. Only once or twice during the long winter season, did he roar out a stentorian, "Go for it, Plummey," when that hero was sitting on the bench.

The Major remained blissfully unaware of Plummey's involvement in high school athletics until he was asked to give a fly-casting exhibition as half-time entertainment in the high school gym.

"Glad to!" he told the high school principal when invited, his wrist already beginning to twitch with desire to get his fly rod back in action.

He arrived at the gym clad in chest waders and

fishing gear just in time to glimpse sweaty players throng-
ing down corridors toward respective locker rooms for
some half-time coaching. Averting his eyes as some
scantily clad nymphet cheerleaders went flouncing past
him, he made himself ready for his act. He concentrated
on readying his rod as though preparing for the fly-
casting championship of the world.

There, of all people, was old Sluter up in the
stands. He bridled a bit at the sight. He couldn't help
but resent the old man for letting that culm of Tsinglee
out of his hands. What a chunk of bamboo! There wasn't
a piece like that left in all of China or even in South
America where the nodes grew farther apart. Sluter
said that he had promised it. To some great fly-fisherman.
He wondered just who it was. Maybe Jack Winton. Or
that guy Polly Rosborough out of Chiloquin, who at
eighty-one was still taking lunkers out of the Williamson.

The Major stood calmly on the sidelines, feeling not
a bit out of place in his outlandish gear, as the little
band finished murdering *Stars and Stripes Forever*, man-
aging a friendly little fake cast now and then up into the
bleachers to honor some acquaintance with his attention.
He even smiled a forgiving smile as the announcer mis-
pronounced his name and stalked out onto the floor.

Major Quillaine did a few warm-up push-ups,
mainly to show the crowd that flycasting was just as
much an athletic event as basketball, then flexed his
rod carefully close to his ear as though tuning up a Stradivarius violin. There may have been a slight titter from

the crowd as the Major summoned up someone from the player's bench with towels to mop up a few beads of perspiration from the floor. Then the crowd was alert but silent as the Major began to cast, and Mr. Sluter was able to follow the Major's whizzing line with his ears.

There was a tiny grimace visible in the set of the Major's jaw as the bursitis in his shoulder caused a twinge of pain, but he soon forgot his handicap as he concentrated on making a showing. In total command, he put his ginger quill through a dazzling repertoire of rolls and dances, using the full length of the floor, now picking up the cadence, now slowing the motion so that it seemed a miracle the fly could stay in the air. Even the doubters were with him now, as though suddenly aware that they were seeing something special, a man in complete control of his art.

Placing a paper cup on the gym floor beneath one basket, he retreated past the center line and once again made the line dance, working it slowly out until the fly was even with the cup, then making the fly do the dance of the mayflies over a stream, sending the line out straight behind him, then gathering power to shoot it forward into a dance above the cup. Up in the band, the drummer began a roll as the Major built to a climax.

The Major was far away. He was on a pool on the Madison, dancing a fly carefully over a ride. Softly, the fly paused and floated down into the cup. A bass drum boomed, and the cup whisked into the air to land at the Major's feet. The Major looked bored, but the crowd leaped to its feet to stamp in approval.

Now the Major took from his pocket a tiny paper cup, the kind restaurants use for jellies and jams, and set it out on the floor. That he could hit such a target seemed impossible to many, but then they were watching one of the great masters. To the crowd, the cup must have seemed only a tiny white speck on the vast seas of the gym floor.

Again the fly sailed out over the room and back over the Major's head. The Major was calm. He had performed the act in Chicago, St. Louis, in London before the Queen, and in the Rose Garden for the President.

The drum began to roll. The Major concentrated hard. He was back on the Laughing Whitefish, hitting a tiny patch of open water between three over-lapping lily pads. The pain in his shoulder had vanished, and the rod, line, and leader seemed extensions of his very soul. One more time, and he would restrain the fly oh so delicately over the cup and let it sail gently down, a tiny parachutist drifting down to hit a tiny circle target on a field.

Just as the Major laid out his back cast for the final grand coup, he looked up to see Plummey Pittock, dressed in basketball uniform, standing in the alley leading to the dressing rooms, watching his performance.

It was the worst cast in the Major's career. On the back cast, the fly sagged almost to the floor, then surged forward with the line to sting the Major right in the

97

back of his thick neck. In disbelief, he continued working his rod, but the hook had dropped to snag itself somewhere in back of his fishing vest. Showman to the end, he reached calmly back, found it with his fingers, then as a nervous titter dared run through the crowd, he pulled it out.

The spot where the boy had stood was now as empty as though Plummey had never existed. Slowly, carefully, the Major once again began to cast, feeding out line, making the fly do precision rolls over the floor. The Major's eyes were mere slits. He was on the Battenkill now, and the last rays of daylight made the water a study of black and silver. The drum was thunder over hemlocked hills. The ginger quill shot forward over the Major's shoulder, stopped high above the tiny cup, and floated down into it. The cymbals clashed as the tiny cup whisked into the air.

Cheers from the crowd. The Major lifted his ragg fishing hat to them, but he could not manage a smile. As he reeled in his line, the band crashed into *Officer of the Day March*. The crowd had forgiven the Major his one small error; indeed there were those who argued that the mishap was contrived, to add drama to his later success. But the Major could not forgive himself. He hated Plummey Pittock as he had never hated anyone in his life.

18

PLUMMEY SAT at Mr. Sluter's workbench and leaned his head upon his arms to rest his eyes. It was Saturday, the opening day of trout season on the Deschutes; but for the first time since he had started fishing with his father, he was missing it. On the bench in front of him lay the component parts of the rod, but Mr. Sluter stubbornly refused to pass on them and declare them ready to assemble. Time and again, the blind man ran his fingers over the bamboo and found fault.

"A little more here; a little more there," the old man advised, running each strip up and down through his fingertips. "They must be perfect or someday a fault might show up to haunt you. It's the wood that possesses the magic, not the glue." And always, when Plummey checked with the micrometer, he found that Mr. Sluter's fingers were correct.

And so, once again, he would set each long, tapering triangle of bamboo back into its special groove in the jig, sharpen the plane until the blade would shave his arm, then carefully whisk off another tiny whisper of wood, following up that operation with a scraping of broken glass and a patient rubbing with steel wool.

He marveled at the old man's quiet confidence, both in him and in the bamboo. There was, perhaps, not a piece like it in the world, yet the old man trusted his hands, just as he trusted that the rod had no hidden defects or dead spots and would turn out to be the finest rod ever crafted.

Plummey would have liked to slip away with the first rod he'd built and try a bit of casting on the Deschutes, but the old man was adamant. "You're still on the big cup," he said. "Wait until you put eight out of ten into the cup of a red oak acorn."

"But that's impossible," Plummey complained. "Even the Major couldn't do that. Why the slightest breeze might throw you off."

"Of course it would sometimes, Plummey, but some day somewhere, you will be casting to the biggest, most important rise of your life, and that tiny bit of accuracy may fool a fish and spell the difference between success and failure."

Soon, floating the fly down into the big cup seemed almost second nature, and the old man graduated him to a tiny jelly cup. On the first cast, the fly floated like thistledown and landed right in the cup.

"Not bad," his mentor admitted as Plummey yelped in excitement. "Now let me see you do it again."

Plummey missed the next twenty tries.

"Check your fly," Mr. Sluter advised. "Maybe the hook is bent or the knot is crooked. Attention to detail; that's the name of the game."

Plummey pulled the fly from the tapered leader, added a new tippet, and tied the fly back on carefully. Again the fly sailed back and forth like a dragonfly, changing direction with lazy grace. Reviewing everything the old man had taught him, he relaxed and concentrated on being perfect. He stared at the cup, wet his lips to determine the direction and degree of the slight breeze, stopped the fly in midair, and let it float downward. Perfect! He moved the cup, cast again, and once more the fly landed on target. "There." He laughed. "Am I ready for the river now?"

"You're ready for the river," Mr. Sluter admitted. "But you'll have to leave your rod behind."

"Why?" Plummey asked.

"Because it would only distract you. This evening, if you'll take me down to the Deschutes, I'll teach you about pools, eddies, currents, feeding periods, insect hatches, things you never had to know much about when you were a bait fisherman."

Plummey felt like retorting that even as a boy he had been able to outfish the townies who came with their fancy Abercrombie and Fitch equipment, but he held his tongue. One of his big learnings had been that Mr. Sluter was very often right and behind his seemingly harsh disciplines was some solid reasoning.

That evening, he walked with Mr. Sluter down along the Deschutes; and once the blind man got his bearings, he seemed to know every deep, every riffle. Through the brush, he walked behind Plummey, with one hand on his shoulder, and at each section of the river, he paused to listen.

Now and then, as he approached some favored spot, he would sit on a windfall and rest, listening to the music of the water he loved. "Tell me, lad. What is it that you see?" he'd ask.

"'Bout a hundred tree swallows cruising up and down the river," he might say.

"Tree swallows? Must be a hatch on. What are they eating?"

"Bugs, I guess."

"Insects, not bugs. What kind are they?"

"Invisible ones."

"They can't be invisible. Get a look at them."

"I can't see anything."

"Wade out into the river. Stare at a patch of water!"

"Hey! An insect flew right up out of the water! Just came right up from the bottom, broke the surface tension, and flew away."

"Describe it!"

"Well, it was—hey! Here's another! It lit on my jacket. It's purplish black, has a forked tail and two clear wings."

"Ahaa! The black drake hatch is on! Look, Plummey, over along the far bank where the river makes a sweep!"

Plummey waded out as far as he could go without being swept away. For a moment he saw nothing, then, just ahead of him, he observed the detritus of a hatch, masses of tiny bodies of little forked-tailed mayflies being swept downstream by the current. Above the pool was a stretch of rapids, and above that a calm, smooth stretch. He spotted a blue haze above the water, and when he waded upstream to check it out, he saw that the air was filled with mayflies dancing up and down over the water as though teasing the fish to leap. Over the water, a dead willow leaned, and its branches wore beards of swarming insects.

Beneath the dance of mayflies, trout rose lazily, slurping one insect from a thousand, hardly breaking the surface. For a time he thought they were only fry; then he saw the rose sides and the big square tail of huge lunkers and realized that a flotilla of large fish lurked just beneath the surface.

In an eddy behind a deadfall pine, a thick scum of spent insects revolved slowly in the gentle current. A song sparrow tested the cake gingerly, found it thick enough to hop upon, and began working the edges for fresh insects. Beak crammed, it flew off to a thicket of wild rose to feed a nestful of babies.

Plummey, of course, had seen similar hatches in past years, but he had been too busy fishing to pay much attention. Now, he became hooked on the whole inter-play of Nature happening before his eyes, and the fish themselves became less important, yet his enjoyment of the experience went far deeper.

"You worked at casting, Plummey, until it became almost second nature. Now you're going to work at being observant until it becomes part of you, until every dimple of an insect on the water registers on your brain yet doesn't interfere with your concentration. Your ultimate purpose, of course, is to land the right fly, at the right instant, in the precise spot, placing an offering exceeding Nature, to entice a huge, wary, overfed denizen to lust over your particular lure in the midst of a spectacular hatch of naturals."

Almost at Plummey's feet, a great shadow of a rainbow trout drifted away from the cutbank to head for the feeding area. The boy's loyalty to Mr. Sluter wavered. At the moment, life seemed terribly short. He wanted to be out there with his rod on the stream right now. Let all this observing Nature jazz come later.

But then he remembered watching the Major from the tree house, seeing that greatest of fly-fishermen doing nothing but sit by the bank of his stream while the hatch peaked, just looking and learning. Old Sluter was a coach preparing him for the championship game, and he would win or lose, perhaps, depending on how well he tended to the practice schedule and game plan.

But still, somehow, it was hard to keep his mind on insect hatches when, only yesterday, he had passed Betty Carlson, blonde tresses tumbling down over her shoulders, wild roses in her cheeks, carrying her own books home from school, and she had given him a certain smile.

19

In LATE JULY, Major Quillaine departed to address the International Symposium on Atlantic Salmon, held in Reykjavic, Iceland. He almost declined the invitation, reasoning that it would take him away from his fishery, but in the end he relented, as Belle had guessed he would.

After all, the President of Iceland, for whom he had once reconstructed a section of salmon river, had asked the Major and his wife to be his guest after the conference to fish the Vididalsa. Before he left home, the Major hired a tough ex-Marine, on leave from the local sheriff's department, to patrol the place and keep everyone off his land, especially Plummey Pittock.

Plummey had heard about the trip from Mr. Sluter and was ecstatic. He had been using his binoculars on the big pool not far from his tree house and had seen a rise that led him to believe the pool contained one whopper of a trout. He thought the rumor of the Major's impending absence too good to be true and stood in back of a large group of well-wishers at the airport, making absolutely sure the Major got on that plane.

Two minutes after it circled the airfield and disappeared to the North, Plummey was on his bicycle peddling hard for Mr. Sluter's house.

He spent four long hours working on the rod, by his diligence doing a sort of penance for what he intended to do, then another two hours practicing his casting in the back yard.

"You're working too hard, Plummey," Mr. Sluter advised, patting him on the shoulder.

I'm glad you said that, Plummey thought to himself. At suppertime he begged leave of Mr. Sluter, saying he had chores to do, and taking the practice rod under his arm, he biked off to his tree house. Plummey had as good as promised Mr. Sluter not to fish the Deschutes until he had completed training, but they had said nothing about the Major's river.

Normally, he might have pranced boldly across the Major's property; but some inner wisdom told him to resort first to his tree house to study the lay of the land. He had not been on his perch five minutes when he detected motion in a patch of willows and a heavyset man strode forth.

"Yipes!" Plummey muttered. "It's Black Belt Beeseley himself. The Major's gone and hired himself a gun!"

Holding his breath, Plummey watched as the deputy, armed with a brace of pistols, went slipping up the valley on patrol, sauntering right on past the big pool. The water flowed silent and undimpled, as though the big trout felt his vibrations along the bank and lay low.

The man seemed nervous, pausing frequently to look about, as if he knew someone spied on him from on high. Like a stump-shy horse, he no sooner determined there were no poachers hiding behind one log, than he picked out another one ahead. With no more conscience than a cow, he trampled through Mrs. Quillaine's new planting of columbines and moved on up the valley.

Plummey calculated his progress. It would take the deputy another half-hour to gain the head of the valley. With his beer belly and run-over-at-the-heels cowboy boots, figure ten minutes to rest and soak his feet, then another half-hour to return. That left a good hour to fish the pool.

He swung down from the tree, took up the fly rod where he had hidden it in the brush, put on the reel, threaded the line through the guides, tied on a brand new tapered leader, and topped that with a Polly Rosborough black drake.

As Plummey approached the pool, a blue-winged teal came rocketing down the stream and almost wiped out the fishing with a landing. Just in time it saw a human and veered away, beating up over the willows. Plummey stayed well back from the water. He longed to waft a fly out over the sweep of current, dropping the drake with pinpoint accuracy just up-riffle from where he imagined the big trout to lie, but, for the moment, loyalty to Mr. Sluter's teaching stayed his hand. Instead of casting, for half an hour he did nothing but savor the biology of the pool.

Getting impatient, he pulled out his pocket watch. There was a chance the deputy might not rest and could already be on his way back. The pool was silent. Perhaps the monster had moved on, or was lying silent in the depths waiting for a hatch.

Riding jauntily on the surface tension of the water, a black drake natural drifted down the stream, wings upright, tail hairs aloft, like rabbit ears antenna alert for TV signals. Below the pool, an eddy caught the insect in a cross current and swamped it. It vanished only to reappear sodden and disheveled below the rapids.

Another perfect drake came sailing right over where the fish must lie. Plummey felt a shiver of excitement, as tension built in his body. He felt a fish just had to rise for that one, but nothing happened. No sign of action anywhere. Maybe he should just try a few casts before the deputy came back, then light out.

Trembling with anticipation, he launched the black drake into the air. The artificial hummed past his ear and out over the water, then back into the blind spot behind him. Using the trick he'd learned spying on the Major, he made it dance over the river. Up and down over the riffle, then back behind him, his left hand governing the slack, keeping tension for a strike. He concentrated hard, with only an occasional glance upstream for the deputy.

The fly settled on the riffle like a puff of eider down, but, not satisfied with the way it rode the water, he pulled the fly off the leader and replaced it with another. Dancing the new fly over the stream, he allowed it to drift a moment, riding high on the current.

There was a sudden false boil as though a fish had come to look at it but changed its mind and retreated. He picked the fly off the pool, dried it with a few casts, then once more let it settle on the water. Another boil, and the fly vanished before his eyes. He set the hook and suddenly a huge fish was racing down the current, stripping out line to the backing. Up to this point, he'd known what he was about, but now he ran into a blind spot in his training. Forgetting himself, he let out a whoop and horsed back on the rod.

His old steel rod and heavy leader might have held, but in that instant the line tightened and the fish raced on; the delicate tip of his bamboo rod burst under the strain; the trout snapped the leader and was gone.

For a long moment, Plummey stared at the rod he'd labored so hard to make. No bringing it back. Moments before, it had been sleek and beautiful. Now eight inches of the tip hung down at right angles. His very first rod, one he could have passed down to his children. Now all he could think of was how to explain matters to Mr. Sluter. He had broken training, abused the blind man's trust. He could think up all sorts of lies, but Mr. Sluter would know the truth the minute he walked into the room.

20

ON THE WAY BACK to Mr. Sluter's house, Plummey conjured up plenty of excuses, none of them with both feet on the truth. But when he entered the house and saw the old man sitting straight in his chair, he blurted out the whole story. "Give me another chance," Plummey said, "and I promise you not to go fishing until you tell me I'm ready."

Mr. Sluter took the rod in his hands as though touching a sick child, moved his gentle fingers up the tip until he came to the break. Instead of being angry, he smiled patiently. "I guess I expected a lot of you, lad, keeping you away from fishing. I'll tell you what, boy. You finish Excalibur, and I promise you we'll spend some evenings on the river together, casting for trout. Small ones, I hope, till you get over the habit of falling over backwards when you get a fish on. And as to fishing the Major's stream, Plummey, why that's his own private fiefdom, not yours. Unless he invites you someday as his guest, I think you should stay away."

Stay off the Major's land? It had never before occurred to him. In his embarrassment, he fidgeted, knowing down deep that Mr. Sluter was right. The whole experience had turned out to be another learning. But that fish! What a monster it was!

Once more he set to work on the Tsinglee cane, Excalibur, no longer impatient to be done, but striving for perfection. When he finally rolled the long strips together, they seemed to fit perfectly. "Fits like a chicken's lip!" he told the old man.

With the blind man at his elbow, he applied the resin and put the rod through the pressure winding machine.

"Better tie it off now and then with strips of rag," the old man suggested, "just to make sure the wrappings don't come loose."

Plummey did as he was told; and when he had finished, he suspended the rod from the ceiling to dry and cure.

As he bicycled back from Mr. Sluter's, he saw Betty Carlson walking down the street ahead of him. Excited at having done so well on making the new rod, he decided he would ride up and talk to her, maybe even tell her about the rod. As he pumped along toward her, he practiced what he might say. "Well, if it isn't Betty Carlson! And how are you today?" Or maybe he would just ride past her without saying anything, pretending he didn't recognize her, then stop up ahead of her as though something was wrong with his bike, and fiddle around with it until she caught up, and get her to hold the wrench for him on the far side of the wheel, while he tightened the other nut.

He had almost caught up with her, when a boy he had never seen before came out of a house, went up to her, and took her books, walking beside her. Plummey went by them both as though they were invisible and didn't slow down until he came to his mother's house.

That night he had a hard time sleeping. He kept worrying about the rod; whether it would cure up without twisting; or whether, when he took the wrapping cords off, there would be hidden defects that would make the rod useless. Then his mind would drift once more to Betty Carlson, and he would conjure up a conversation with her. Once he even dared imagine he was teaching her to cast with a fly rod and had to stand behind her with his arms around her to help her. And boy, was she a slow learner!

He had several paying jobs around town to catch up on and that helped him keep his mind (and hands) off Excalibur as it cured. He was shaking like a leaf when he took it down from its hook and, with Mr. Sluter's help, removed the bindings, scraped off all traces of glue, and finished it off with a rubbing of fine steel wool. There was a slight twist in the long, gleaming piece, but they straightened the wood by heating it and holding it in position as it cooled.

From a drawer, Mr. Sluter brought out a package wrapped in soft rags, from which he unwound a handle of finest Spanish cork and a reel mount of silver, exquisitely engraved with leaping trout. The silver was black with age, but the old man soon had it gleaming.

"Been saving these for years," Mr. Sluter said. "Never found a rod before that deserved them." He rolled up his sleeves and sat down beside Plummey on the bench to help him assemble the rod and wrap on a set of gleaming guides with threads of shimmering red silk.

When at last the reel mount and handle slid into place, Plummey could hardly contain himself for joy. "It's gorgeous," he said with a chuckle to Mr. Sluter. "I guess it's got to be the prettiest rod in the whole world!"

Mr. Sluter sat quietly on the bench holding the rod in his hands, caressing it, memorizing every line, flexing it carefully as he checked every inch of the rod for faults.

"We're in luck," he said. "There's not a dead spot in the length of her." In his hands the rod trembled with life. "I'd like to sit here holding it forever." Mr. Sluter smiled. "But let's get her varnished up. It will take long enough as it is to cure." He handed Plummey a delicate brush and from a shelf took down a small jar of dark varnish. Soon the gleaming rod hung from the ceiling, and the two friends went tiptoeing from the cabin lest one speck of dust be wafted through the air to mar that otherwise perfect job.

For the month of August, Plummey left the varnished rod hanging to dry and cure, but he came in often just to stand and admire his handiwork. Ever since he had broken the tip of his own rod, he had been practicing with Mr. Sluter's. Once it had seemed like the epitome of rods, but now as he took Excalibur down from its hook, there seemed to be a life in the piece flowing not from his hands but from the wood itself. It was the stuff of greatness.

Carefully, one day, he mounted the little Hardy reel on the silver mount, fitted the line through the gleaming guides, tied on a tapered leader, followed with a Silver Doctor, then moved to the back yard where he stood quietly a moment, before daring to roll the fly into the air. It was as though the clumsy artificial had suddenly been given life and now flew about in the air trying to attract a mate.

Mr. Sluter sat on his garden bench and listened to the sounds, concentrating like a composer at the debut of his first symphony. The Silver Doctor flew easily, pausing in midflight to track back the way it had come.

"Come on, Mr. Sluter," Plummey said, bursting with pride. "Stand up here and give it a try!"

The old man shook his head. "I'm happy for you, Plummey. No one else but you should touch it. It might confuse the wood. And if I tried it, somehow I'd seem disloyal to the good old rod I've had these many years."

From the Silver Doctor, Plummey went to a Parmachene Belle, to a tiny stone fly, then to a bumblebee, and finished with a black gnat. Each fly, however it varied from the rest, moved with the same uncanny grace.

Once school had started in the fall, Plummey had to fight for time to practice casting. If he could not make it during daylight hours, he dropped by Mr. Sluter's house on his bike and stood in the half light of the back yard, casting by the light of the cabin windows, turning the rod into an extension of himself. Often he wished there were others his age with whom he could talk rods, flies, and fish, but in that small high school there didn't seem to be another with his interests.

One Saturday, when there was only a week of angling season left, and Plummey was wondering whether or not Mr. Sluter ever intended to let him fish, the old man groped for his outfit. "Come on, lad. It's time. Time to go with me down to the Deschutes and learn what that rod was really made to do. Catch fish."

"You mean that, Mr. Sluter?" He picked up his gear and was out the door before the old man could change his mind.

Plummey led him to the Great Pool, at the end of the Lower Pittock, where they stood just beyond the Major's boundary at the point where his stream poured down through the fish screens back into the Deschutes. The Major's system produced so much more food than its denizens could consume that the surplus poured into the Great Pool, making the wild trout fat and sassy.

Side by side, the two companions waded out into the chill waters of the river. "You ought to see the cotton-woods, Mr. Sluter," Plummey said. "It's as though the whole bottom has turned to gold overnight."

He watched over the old man like a mother hen with one lone chick, but he need not have worried. His blind friend seemed able to sense the stronger currents with his toes and stayed safely a few inches from the deeper channels. A smile of contentment warmed the man's face as he cast the riffles of his boyhood.

"Downstream a little, Mr. Sluter," Plummey advised. "The Major's stream has changed things a little from what you remember. It's at the mouth of the Major's river now that the trout come to feed. Left, no, just a hair, and eight inches further out. There! Right on. Let her drift."

A twelve-inch rainbow took Mr. Sluter's fly. "Now," said the old man happily, reading the splash. "You see how I raised the tip of my rod? Just enough to set the hook. Now I feel him making his run downstream. See how I hold my arms high and the rod tipped slightly back? The force goes down the whole rod and into my arms. I don't need eyes to tell he's running wild! Not a very big fish, but he knows how to use the current. I'll let him strip some backing off the reel. Now! Slowly, gently, I start the discipline. I apply a touch of pressure on the line with my left hand and turn him. Inch by inch, I'll work him back this way."

Mr. Sluter had caught and released a dozen small trout when Plummey began to concentrate on his own casting and caught his first trout on the new rod. He played to a generous rise and hooked him well. The big trout shot out of the pool into the rapids, pulling out line and backing as the reel screamed in protest. Plummey had a flash of helpless terror that he'd played this scene before, and the rod tip was about to break in a thousand pieces under pressure.

He held his arms up high, splashing downstream after the fish. The swift current almost swept him off his feet, and the rocks, covered with green slime, were treacherous. The rod bowed in one long, graceful arc, but the big trout slowed, and the fragile leader held. No more horsing back the way he'd been able to do with his dad's old telescope rod. But still he was so uptight about the chance of breaking that precious rod, he now wished he were back in Mr. Sluter's back yard.

Little by little, he brought the fish up the current. "He's coming a little now," he advised Mr. Sluter.

"You're doing fine!" The old man laughed, enjoying Plummey's adventure as his own. "Play him until he's too tired to wiggle. Many's the overeager fisherman that's lost his prize."

Trying to shake the hook, the trout leaped high, his sides gleaming rose in the sunlight. Splashing back into the current, he tried another downstream run. Again the rod tip held; Excalibur had passed the test!

Soon the big trout lay on his side exhausted in the shallows. "My first fish on a fly," Plummey bragged. "Four pounds, Mr. Sluter, if he's an ounce." He reached down slowly so as not to startle the fish, wet his fingers, then unhooked the fly. Softly, he brought the fish about into the current, letting the flowing water oxygenate the rose gills. The trout made a few half-hearted sweeps with his tail, then discovered his freedom and streaked for deep water.

The old man listened to the sounds and smiled. "You turned him loose?" he said.

"Yeah," Plummey replied. "I reckon that's what Major Quillaine would have done."

21

MAJOR QUILLAINE hurried through the front door of his ranchhouse, rid himself of Belle and their suitcases, shed his traveling clothes to lie like puddles on the floor, slipped into his chest waders, and headed out the back door toward his stream. All day long, during the flights from Iceland, he'd suffered a premonition that things weren't as he left them. In his mind's eye, the Virgin Queen didn't seem to be in her pool; and, sure enough, when, at last, he stood on the rocky outcropping and looked down into the clear, cold water, he couldn't find her anywhere.

First he checked under the cutbank, where often her big, square tail could just be seen fluting in the current, then under the sunken log, where, if she were in residence, both nose and tail would be exposed. Moving down around the pool, he waded out into the riffles, where his footfalls should have sent her streaking for cover.

No fish there! And some fading footprints in the damp soils along the edge of the stream! Fearing the worst, he shook his fist at Plummey's tree house. It just wasn't fair! He went down the stream in a long trot, starting to perspire in his waders, peering in pools, stomping undercut banks, searching in vain for the huge trout. Down to the end of the stream, where the water poured through into the Deschutes, then upstream again past the Queen's favorite haunt.

He cursed himself for going to Iceland. Maybe that stupid deputy had seen her in the pool and taken her with bait, or, even worse, a spear. Ahead of him, a great blue heron, intent on frog or minnow, waited until the last possible instant to leap into the air, its gutteral, croaking melancholy adding somehow to his own severe depression.

Just ahead of him, in his absence, a beaver had felled a large aspen into the stream, and the swirl of water had created a new pool he hadn't planned. It reminded him of one he'd seen once up near Great Slave Lake. It was on an unnamed stream he'd come across while camped along the shores of the big lake, and as he balanced on an aspen log, he'd noticed that special pool and wondered what kind of fish it held. A black gnat delivered just above the mass of beaver cuttings had—

Just then a huge gout of icy water drenched the Major and snapped him back to the present. Beneath his feet, the Virgin Queen had been lazing in the shallows and now shot upstream toward deeper water. Her

wide back glistened above her wake, and her vermillion speckles on a field of orange and cream gleamed like tiny jewels in the setting sun. He whooped his excitement, and the outburst seemed only to add speed to her flight. She was gone as suddenly as she had appeared, lost in the murky depths beneath the beaver tree.

The Virgin Queen! Alive and well! She hadn't vanished forever, only moved upstream a few hundred yards, perhaps because something had frightened her, or maybe only because the beaver tree had fallen across the stream above and was filtering the drift of surface insects, making for leaner times in the pool immediately below.

She seemed wilder now than he remembered. No trace left of the young female he'd planted who would tolerate him watching from above like a Sunday visitor at a trout hatchery. Had something spooked her during his absence, or was it only the new surroundings that made her uncomfortable or wary out of her old familiar beat? In his wet clothes, the Major shivered, but whether from cold or excitement he did not know. The Warm Springs Indians were predicting early snows. Already the tops of the Cascades were ringed with white.

The Major smiled to himself. All winter long the Queen would be safe and snug in her own stream, feeding and growing. Already she had moved on well past the record mark, and, by spring . . . Well, it would be time to take her and register her mark upon the record books.

He moved on up the river on his rounds. By now the scars left by earth movers and bulldozers had healed, and the vegetation looked as though it had sprung up naturally.

He felt good about his project. Maybe he did have "trout on the brain," as his neighbors claimed, but there were other things in Nature he loved, too. And when you built a wetlands of any sort, you created a total system, from the food chains born of water to the flora and fauna leaping up along the shores.

A winter wren piped plaintively from a pile of juniper brush. If he and Belle hadn't piled that brush one summer afternoon and avoided the impulse to be neat, there wouldn't be a winter wren hopping about in it now, would there?

Earlier the warblers that came traveling up the can-yon in the fall, instead of hurrying through, seemed to find the new source of food and shelter intriguing and stayed on for weeks beyond their time. The Major didn't spend a lot of time looking at birds, but he managed to count more than a hundred and fifty different species, a good share of which, but for his project, would not have bothered to stop off at the old Pittock farm.

Some food, of course, had been there. Water, cover, and privacy had made a difference. Funny, the Major mused one day as he eased the upper head gate down a bit for winter. The winds seem to blow across everyone's land whether welcome or not, but wildlife comes best to those properties where it is loved.

In the pool below him, a mink nosed along the shore for crayfish, and a beaver, perhaps sensing the declining water level, came out through a tunnel beneath the bank and floated with the current as though making sure the stream was still going to run. As the Major moved on down the watercourse, the beaver smacked its tail in alarm, and dove, leaving a telltale wake of bubbles as it swam underwater toward the safety of its lodge.

As he hiked on toward home, the skies darkened ominously with storm clouds, and a cold fog rose from the stream and seemed to hang at the level of the treetops. By the time the Major reached his house, it was snowing in earnest, and already the ground was white. With his toe, he dug down to the frozen earth as though to re-assure himself that summer had once been there.

22

It was the last the Major saw of the ground until spring.
Storm after storm blew in off the Pacific, inundating
the coastal regions of Oregon with rain. As the moisture-
laden clouds were ramped to higher elevations by the
towering Cascades, snow dumped over the pine and fir
covered mountains burying lesser trees with a heavy
pack. It was a winter when summer cabins lost their
roofs, giant trees that had braved the storms for centu-
ries went down, and even the giant snowblowers could
not keep the mountain passes open for long.

For a time, farmers and fishermen alike celebrated
the snow pack, toasting a dream of ample water supplies
for power, agriculture, and recreation. But the snowpack didn't stop at plenty. Day after day, the snow kept
falling, choking the rivers with slush, breaking branches
and power lines alike. On ranches there were no longer
fences, only vast snow plains and herds running in common.

Soil Conservation Service readings of the snowpack

showed first a hundred eighty percent of normal moisture, then two hundred. For coastal streams spring flooding was accepted as inevitable. North and south, families spent their spare time filling sandbags.

And yet, no one really worried about the Deschutes. For much of its way from the Cascades to the Columbia, the river ran through deep, ancient canyons, well able to handle the river in flood. Only the Major was concerned. The old Pittock Place lay on the river plain, and the old gravelly soils and giant boulders stood as mute testimony that the Deschutes could go on a rampage. He and Belle could move up the rimrocks for safety, and they would not mourn for long the loss of that battered but snug Pittock farmhouse. But what of the Queen? What would happen to the Queen?

There was a day in mid-January when temperatures crashed to thirty below zero; schools were closed; and the blue wood smoke hung heavy along the farmlands above the Deschutes.

The Major's stream froze over, and only the purl of tumbling water beneath the ice told that the stream still ran. In spite of the bitter cold, the Major roamed his land, watching, waiting, for what he did not know, but filled with a nameless dread that some accident would happen before spring.

It was no use, Belle knew, to try to persuade him to stay indoors. Often she wished to herself that the great trout was gone, and she could have her marriage back. But she was patience herself. She saw to it that the Major had his gloves, his scarf, and carried a candle in his pocket and a small Thermos of coffee. She could not have worried more about a child.

Night after night, new records were broken in seven of the western states. Even the mighty Deschutes was tamed by ice.

"This cold can't last forever," Mr. Sluter observed from the wisdom of years. "But just the same, Plummey, I'm mighty grateful to you for all that firewood."

What with people's chores, frozen pipes, neglected woodpiles, and stalled automobiles, Plummey had never been so busy.

That night, as swiftly as it had all begun, a new weather front moved in from off the Pacific. The cold moderated; rain fell at high elevations. Far up along the Deschutes and its tributaries, ice began to break up and move.

As long as the ice cakes moved freely down the Deschutes, the Major did not worry. He sat and watched the big flat white barges of ice bobbing by on their way to the Columbia and was relieved to see them drifting along so easily. Rain pelted his face. He turned his cold, wet cheeks from the weather, frightening a feeding junco, who fluttered up into a willow and sat for an instant, feathers stuck on backwards by the wind, its bedraggled tail like the ribs of a blown-out umbrella. Only when it was too dark to see did the Major give up his lonely vigil and seek shelter.

Early the next morning, as the Major and Belle hiked along the Deschutes, he noticed that the ice, which had been coursing smoothly past only moments before, had ceased to move, and the water level in the river was dropping rapidly.

"Run!" he shouted to Belle. "Head for the rim-rocks! There must be an ice jam up the canyon!"

Safe atop the rims, they hurried forward until they reached a vantage point overlooking the Major's diversion, and from there they could look on up the canyon and see a long lake forming behind a plug of shattered ice. The dam held for only a few more minutes, then, as water began to cascade over the lip, the whole ice barricade gave way and swept down the canyon with an awesome roar.

Roots in the air, a forest of junipers did slow motion cartwheels until they were swallowed by the relentless ice pack. Even the giant cottonwood by the diversion, which had been old long before there were Pittocks on the land, shuddered and fell, shattering like so many matchsticks to be buried in the mass.

Thrusting out ahead of the advancing wall of ice and water, a great muddy tongue licked up everything in its way, collapsing the trash-catcher as though it were a child's toy, then shoving the head gates before it, pushing them high up against the base of the rims, where it abandoned them half buried in dirt and talus debris. As the ice plug moved out of the canyon, a flood of muddy water spilled around both ends and inundated the Pittock Bottom.

The Major sat beside his wife, his face as gray and forbidding as the lava rocks about him. Somewhere down in that torrent, the Virgin Queen must be fighting for her life against powerful torrents, perhaps hugging the bottom to avoid the great, grinding, buckling slabs of ice.

The ordeal was soon over. Once the plug had been by-passed by the torrent, the water began to recede from the land. As soon as he dared, the Major slid on down the hillside, then waded in, checking each stranded pool for the Queen. All along the wreck of his stream were puddles of pond life, seeking safe haven in backwaters of silted water and weeds. Soon the Deschutes was back in its channel, and the Major's stream was nearly dry, but there was no sign of the great trout.

He stood with Belle amid the ruin of his dreams. "She's gone," he said. "Down the main river, ground into so much fish meal, or buried in silt. Who knows? And with her went my hopes for a record." He nodded toward the wonderful stream he had built with such painstaking care. "Look about you," he said. "It's a mess."

"We can start over," Belle said. "Why the place will heal up in no time. By spring the columbines will be coming up, and the aspens will be in new leaf. The head gates look to be in good shape; just a little out of place is all, like maybe a quarter of a mile. A few yards of concrete and the whole system will be better than new. A flood like that wouldn't happen again in a hundred years. More years than we have to worry about anyway."

"The Queen is gone," the Major said, as though that were reason enough to call it quits.

"Well, so she is," Belle said. "So what? By spring, bet you have the whole river flowing again. You'll be surprised at what survives. And then you can find another trout. Maybe it won't shoot up as dramatically as the Queen, but with all the trout food in your river system, it will be a record-breaker for sure."

As though in quiet acceptance of Belle's reasoning, the Major picked up the broken top of a cottonwood and began dragging it out of the stream bed. Somehow his momentum wasn't quite going yet, but it was a start.

Moving down along the empty streambed, still nursing the tiny hope that the Queen might be landlocked in one of the tiny bayous, the Major felt better when he had inspected the whole scene. Plenty of cleaning up to do; debris littered the plain. But the lower screens were intact. The water had cut around them, and a few hours with a bulldozer would restore the lower system.

In the bottom of one of the pools, a family of beaver huddled together. Major Quillaine and his wife herded them up over the bank and headed them toward the Deschutes. It didn't take the beaver long to figure out where they were bound, and they were soon lost in the brush along the river.

"They'll be back one day," the Major said, becoming more positive. "They'll be back as soon as we turn water down the system." Already he was making plans. He'd need a crew to put the head gates in, and he'd make a new trash-catcher with refinements over the first one. The rest was clean-up work. In time the river would once more run through the Pittock Bottom.

23

APRIL CAME, and it was as though Nature was a bit embarrassed by her excesses of the winter past. Though the waters were higher than normal, they were orderly, with cool weather in the Cascades releasing no more meltwater than the regular channels could handle. There were a few disgruntled homeowners, mainly transplanted Californians, who had built too close to the streams and saw their basements inundated, but most folks along the waterways felt relieved that they had not been dealt worse.

For a time that winter, the Major had done some moping along the Deschutes, staring for hours at the turbulent waters, hoping against hope that the Virgin Queen would somehow show herself in a spectacular leap. But when day after day produced nothing more for him than low morale, he threw himself into his restoration project.

The trash-catcher was first. The Major rebuilt it

with improvements, so no longer did it tremble and shake like a go-go dancer with the heaves. Then came the head gates, set in heavier concrete, with a special dike beside it that would break in case of flood, yet leave the breast-works intact.

By mid-May, water was once more running through the system, wild rice was emerging along margins and quiet stretches, a few lily pads were breaking the surface of the water to flutter in the wind, and beneath them were more a-coming. Each bend sported a trio of courting ducks, leaping often from the water with great fanfare to fly their nuptial flights high over the cottonwoods and return splashing to their favorite pool. The first colum-bines were pushing up through the bare alluvial fans in Belle's grove. And as the Major predicted, the beavers were back in their lodges.

The same trout farmer who had produced the Vir-gin Queen advised the Major over the phone that he had just the fish for him, another specimen eastern brook trout female, even more impressive than the first, and would hold her for a small deposit. Except for the loss of the Queen, the Major thought that things had never been quite so good.

To admirers around town, it seemed that the Major had pretty much returned to being his old self. Often he could be seen traipsing down Main Street in his chest waders, casting a friendly fly across the street at a friend, or cornering an acquaintance along the block, regaling him with a tale of how he had caught this monster or that on the Madison or the Whatever. His bursitis? Well, it was still there, true enough, but being resigned to it made the affliction a little easier to bear.

Deep down, his resolve to claim his much-deserved place in the record books was still as firm as ever; but, as far as he could determine, that auspicious event was still two years down the pike, depending on just how big the new Queen turned out to be when he bought her, and how fast, under the optimum conditions of the Major's stream, she could grow.

One Friday evening, when Belle and the Major had finished dealing with the emergencies on the place and could find time to relax, the Major took a fly rod and gear and wandered down with Belle past the discharge of his system into the Deschutes, determined to try a few casts over the Great Pool.

It was a time of magic. Overhead the snipe were winnowing; nighthawks were wheeling and booming; deep within the alder and ozier thickets chats were scolding; night herons were working the river margins; and mayflies were dancing over smooth, darkling waters, while already a host of pan-sized rainbows were working the backwaters to a silver froth.

Leaving Belle watching from the bank, he waded into the river. The cold water felt good rushing past his warm waders. He moved out past waist level as the pressure of the water firmed about him, driving his waders tight against him like a rubber skin and caressing his old body with a hundred quarreling crosscurrents.

Upstream, downstream, as far as he could see there

were no other fishermen to spoil his concentration. Except for his own concrete abutments, already nearly hidden from view by moss and vegetation, he noted with satisfaction that the great Deschutes, at this point, probably looked as it had for hundreds of years.

Taking his fly box out of his vest, he opened it and was inspecting the neat rows of flies to match those slender mayflies of the hatch, when the box slipped from his grasp, spun away into the swift current, and went bobbing saucily down the Deschutes. The Major cursed himself for being so clumsy and was even madder when he discovered that he had no spare flies drying, either on his hatband or on the lambswool patches of his vest.

Backing slowly away from the current, feeling for solid bottom with his heels, he was about to leave the river when, suddenly, what appeared to be a big beaver sounded an alarm, smacking the surface of the great pool with his broad tail. From where he stood, the Major could feel the spray.

Wary of the currents, he turned slowly to look, but already the animal had dived deep, leaving only surface bubbles and a retreating wake.

The Major was almost ready to turn away, when, from the bottom of the pool, he caught the flash of a giant fish headed for the surface, gathering speed for a leap. Breaking the calm, a huge brook trout soared through the air, shook off a blood-sucking lamprey in mid-leap, and fell back with a crash that sent waves over the top of the Major's waders.

The man lurched backwards in surprise, lost his

footing on the slippery rocks, and fell over, half swimming, half crawling into the shallows where Belle offered him a hand. Ignoring her, he pulled himself up on the gravel bar with his elbows like a walrus hauling out on a reef. For a long moment he lay letting the water drain, looking out on the Great Pool, studying the water as though he had not memorized every riffle of it years before. Then a smile began at the square corners of his mouth and spread into laughter. He hadn't a fly on his person, and out in that froth of water was none other than the Virgin Queen.

It would be the longest night of his life, but, come morning, the Major would be back on the Great Pool with a fresh assortment of flies, ready to catch what had to be the largest brook trout in North America.

24

Before daylight, Plummey dropped by to take Mr. Sluter down to the Great Pool fishing, but, due to a bout with rheumatism, the resolve of evening had vanished. The boy took Excalibur and went alone.

He was on a real high. Yesterday, in school, who should be transferring her books to the locker right next to his but Betty Carlson. She smiled at him and blushed, and some pent-up dam within him had burst in a flood. "HowjaliketogoflyfishingwithmesometimedownontheDeschutes,Betty?"

"What?"

"Howjaliketogofishingwithmesometimedownonthe-Deschutes?"

As he gulped hard, trying to get his breath, she smiled easily as though she had been planning this exchange for a long time. "Great!" she said. "I've got some new fly patterns my dad and I just tied up; I'm dying to try them out."

The school baseball hero grabbed her by the hand then and dragged her down the hall; but when she finally disappeared around the corner, she was still looking back over her shoulder at Plummey, smiling.

The Deschutes was higher than he liked, but it was steady, and the trout should be hungry after the long winter; he anticipated a good morning. It was not, however, foolish young trout that interested him. As he had been telling Mr. Sluter, down in the Great Pool he had seen a brook trout jump that was truly awesome.

Had it been a rainbow, he might have assumed that it was on its way upstream to spawn; but brook trout had a firm sense of home, and he sensed that the monster might live in the Great Pool. He had seen that fish again, nosing about the base of the screens where the Major's stream entered the top of the Pool. He had a sneaking suspicion that perhaps the big trout might have washed in from the Major's system and might even be the big monster that broke the tip of his rod.

Just short of the Great Pool, he paused in the half-darkness to fit his line through the guides and tie on a fresh new tapered leader. A light fog was rising from the river, melding into the air; and in the gloom, he could only partially make out the osprey's nest high in the dead cottonwood above his head. He could hear the fish hawks, however, already up and about their housekeeping; and once, as his pants brushed a patch of willow, the parents hurled a few high-pitched invectives down upon his head.

The melted snow water called for insulated waders, but since Plummey did not own a pair, he had to be content with working himself into a good position to cast. He climbed out on the fog-slickened promontory of rocks that thrust out into the upper reaches of the pool, then, once he was in position, he sat quietly, waiting for dawn, staring into the silver-gray, coursing water as though trying to determine the hatch.

Several times during the night, the Major had gotten out of bed to check his equipment. He was not about to risk losing the Queen by lack of attention to detail. Again and again, he inspected rod, line, backing and leader and tried out his hooks so often on his thumb for sharp, he had to get a Band-aid out of the bathroom cabinet. Long before dawn, he rose, cooked himself some breakfast, slipped into his chest waders, took his gear, and headed out into the darkness.

It was almost daylight when Major Quillaine arrived at the Great Pool. A light fog was rising from the river, limiting visibility. Above the roar of tumbling water, he heard the ospreys shrieking at some intruder beneath their nest, then they were quiet as the animal passed on.

Like a blue heron getting ready to fish, the Major waded out into the water and found his position, then stood motionless, letting the slurry settle around his green rubber legs. There was not much happening in the way of a hatch. Dimly he could make out a few half-drowned Baetis from the river above, drifting across the pool. They swung by him on the drift without attracting so much as a swirl, then gathered momentum as they shot the riffles and were gone.

He pictured the Queen lying tight along the bottom and wondered if a Baetis nymph, fished deep past her nose might not take her. But somehow, on this great occasion, he could not depart from purity. With a nymph, fished deep, he'd miss the excitement of the visual, the great leap at his command that would carry her into the air with a dry fly clinging to her lip. Taking up a tiny, dark mayfly, he tied it on his leader and blew on the hackles for luck. Rolling it out on the water to check its ride, he caught it up again, tugging on the knot with his fingers to straighten it, but careful not to compress the body.

The Major was about to cast again, when a bit of motion from the rocks above the pool caught his eye. He froze. Just over the escarpment, he could see the tip of a fly rod moving back and forth, back and forth, and from that tip flowed a line moving wondrously, as gracefully as any he had seen.

On any other occasion, the Major would have quit the pool rather than to share it with another; but the thought of leaving the Virgin Queen for someone else to take was more than he could stand.

That was no rank amateur out there. Whoever was fishing beyond the rocks was really laying out a line like a master. But the Major told himself he was on his home turf. Let the stranger fish those upper reaches; he himself would fish where only hours before he had seen the Queen. He glanced once more toward where he had seen the rod working above the rocks, but the fog had lowered, hovering over the sweep of water like a shroud.

Out at the limit of his vision, the Major saw a swirl, but it was from a large rainbow and not the giant brookie. He avoided the spot with his fly. Instead, he sailed the tiny artificial over the riffle where he himself, if he were the Queen, would choose to lie. The cast felt good, and riding high on its hackles, the fly followed the same drift pattern as the naturals. He gave the fly a slight tweak as though it were considering flying away.

A flight of mergansers drilled through the mists, leaving a swirl of fog. Once again he could see that elegant rod moving back and forth. Fearing to miss a strike, he could only manage a glance when his own fly was in the air. A bamboo by the action, and all one piece. You didn't see those often. Whoever was using it was as unusual as the rod. Couldn't be anyone local. The stranger out there on the point had chosen that spot either because he had torn his waders or was afraid to be swept away by unfamiliar currents. It would never have occurred to the Major that a flycaster that talented might not own waders.

On the other side of the rock, it hadn't taken Plummey long to figure out that there was another fisherman on the pool and that the Major was the man. Well, as far as he could tell, he'd been there first this morning, and he wasn't about to abandon the pool to the Major.

Besides, the older man was tackling waters only some-one with chest waders could fish. Actually, the Great Pool was big enough for two. Plummey concentrated hard on his presentation, trying to remember everything Mr. Sluter had told him.

Way he had it figured, the trout might be feeling homesick for the Major's personal stream and might just be hanging around tasting familiar water right there where the incoming stream dumped its load of food. He supposed the trout to be an eager eater, preferring first choice at the drift fluting into the pool, making instant decisions where a less active fish might hang back in lesser currents.

Plummey did not know the name of the fly he was using; it was an olive drab job from a batch Mr. Sluter had provided and seemed to imitate the hatch. Below him where the rocky point deflected the current, a few small trout had been feeding, but they ceased suddenly as though some monster of the deep had driven them to cover. He wished the fog would lift; often now his fly landed so far out on the stream, it was hard to manage the drift.

By now the hackles were damp, and he replaced the sodden fly with a fresh one, a gray hackle with gold body and scarlet tail. Maybe the brookie would mistake that red tail for a succulent emerging egg case.

On the first cast, as the fly drifted to the race and sprinted away on the current, Plummey caught a flash of pearl. A big trout had mooned it, then retreated to the depths. His stomach turned a back flip; for a moment he retrieved his fly while he sucked in some deep breaths to steady his shaking hands. He put off casting by checking his knots and testing the hook. He figured now that he knew where the big fish was lying, not straight with the river channel, but headed off at an angle, where some hidden, underwater obstruction was deflecting the current. To better the angle of his cast, Plummey moved a little farther out on the point.

Conscious that by now his back must be fully exposed to the Major's line of sight, he rolled his fly a little awkwardly into the air, hoping it wouldn't snag on some upstart willow in the hazard area behind him. A light breeze challenged him, swirling the fog and lifting it up through a chimney between the cottonwoods. As he powered it forward, Plummey tried to compensate, but the wind died mischievously before he had completed his cast. Again and again the tiny fly sailed out over the water as the boy eyed a target spot where he wanted the fly to land.

All of a sudden it felt sweet. He braked the gray hackle yellow and let it float down like a tiny helicopter auto-rotating, deflecting just the tiniest bit as it hit the air current immediately above the water's surface. For one instant, the fly settled on the race and poised; then suddenly the race itself exploded into a burst of fish-flung spray. Powering upwards from hidden depths, the giant brook trout slashed at the fly and carried on upwards into the air.

Remembering his training, Plummey lifted the tip of Excalibur slightly to take up slack in the leader and seemed to hear a sharp tick as if a hook point were striking cartilage. Sliding head first into the current, the trout went slashing across the pool, heading for the churning rapids down below.

The Major first knew of the strike when the figure on the point let out a whoop like an Indian and whirled toward him. His arch enemy, Plummey Pittock himself, was suddenly bursting down upon him, holding his fly rod high, leaping from rock to rock, teetering wildly as the huge trout kept pulling him off balance. With his line and most of his backing stripped from his reel, the boy was just split seconds away from losing his fish.

"Help me, Major Quillaine!" the boy pleaded. "Tell me what to do! I'm kind of green in all this!"

"Impertinent pup!" the Major muttered to himself, sitting down in the icy torrent to avoid losing an ear as Plummey's line slashed across his neck. The current caught him up and began rolling him downstream like a half-empty beer keg. He was back suddenly fishing the Lamoille, begging his Uncle Mac to tell him how to handle a huge German brown. Looking back with blistering clarity, fifty years into his past, he saw the rod. Not the delicate bamboo he hoped he remembered, but a telescope of an iron rod with guides lined with red garnet. He tried to fight off the vision, but it wouldn't go away. Sputtering to the surface, he got his feet beneath him and heaved toward shore, lurching forward against the current and hoisting out on a gravel bar.

Tennis shoes flying, splashing down through slippery shallows after his prize, Plummey managed to keep up as the big fish bolted down through one hell sluice after another, using the massive force of the water to its advantage.

The Major was back on the Laughing Whitefish. Nineteen thirty-four, and there wasn't much money around. Yet Mushrat John, who eked out an existence trapping up near the Peter White Camp, had sold off two dozen rats and a prime mink pelt to buy him his first fly rod. He'd taken that whopping big rainbow on the marsh near his camp, but it had been John who coached him, John who told him where to cast, John who paddled the canoe.

"Major Quillaine!" Plummey called. "What do I do now?"

The Major was a truer champion than he knew. He went chuffing up the bank through a beaver run, water sloshing over the tops of his waders and shooting out through a dozen rock tears in the rubber. He stood on high ground at last and turned to take command. "After him!" the Major shouted, snapping back to reality. "Keep that rod high, and the next time he hits a pool, ease him into the backwater." The Major had eyes for the fish alone, refusing to look at Plummey.

"I—I think I've gone and lost him!" Plummey moaned, feeling nothing but a dead, unmoving weight on his line.

"Nonsense!" the Major snapped. "I can see your line move. Hang in there! Keep up the pressure; don't give an inch of slack, or she'll spit the hook! She's in a sull."

The Major was back in his boyhood fishing for goggle-eyed rock bass on Deer Lake. The red garnet guides on the telescope pole gleamed in the late afternoon sun like a maharaja's rubies. He was proud of that rod. He had seen it one Saturday afternoon in Richard's Sport Shop and had counted out all his pennies, but still come up with two dollars short in having enough to buy it. Otto Schwenky, the manager, had caught him with his nose pressed against the glass case, and, perhaps to keep from having to clean the showcase, had let him have the rod with the promise of some chores after school.

. Plummey's arms ached from holding them high. Keeping the rod bent, he rested his elbows against his chest, then managed to retrieve some of the line with his left hand, letting the slack pool around his feet.

"Not too much," the Major warned. "Any second now she might take another run."

The Queen came suddenly out of her sull and hurtled toward Plummey, throwing slack.

"Run backwards," the Major shouted, dancing up and down. "Take up slack, boy! Take up slack!"

Charging backwards, Plummey tripped over a piece of driftwood and fell on his back, but still managed to hold onto the fish.

"Atta boy," the Major cheered. "On your feet! Quickly now before she can start another run!" For the first time, the Major seemed to scrutinize the rod, now bent into a glorious bow as it held the line taut. It seemed to him he had never seen a more beautiful piece.

He saw, suddenly, the hand of old Sluter in the scene. He'd triumphed, the blind man had. Taken a local wormie and, by Hell, he'd coached him into a fly-fishing fool! And that great piece of cane he'd coveted for years, why Sluter and the boy had turned it into a great one-piece rod!

"Get with her, lad!" the Major shouted as once more the Queen began to move.

Shoulders cramping, Plummey concentrated on the fish, matching his speed to her forward progress as she moved upstream again. He let out a bit more line, but kept enough dragging to handle a run.

"Watch out!" the Major coached. "She might turn back down one of those chutes. Easy now! Watch her close! Keep the tip of your rod high so she doesn't find a snag and break your leader."

A faint sliver of larceny embedded itself in the Major's heart. He had raised that fish himself for the record book, and now it was the boy who would triumph. Entirely too young to deserve such an honor. Maybe someday, but not now. Might ruin him as a fisherman. Just one mistake, and the fight would be over. Still plenty of strength left in the big trout. There was a sunken log over there that the boy couldn't possibly see, and the Queen was angling toward it. Any moment now, he sensed she might make a run, dart under the log, and break that fragile leader. And then—she would be free! In a few weeks, she would be ready to strike again.

"No No! No!" the Major shouted suddenly, bow-

145

ing his head and clutching his two fists against his temples as though in pain. If he destroyed this moment for the boy, there would be no bringing it back. And suppose he did catch the Queen next week, next month, next year. He would only release her unrecorded, the way he had done all the rest.

"No, what? Major, am I doing it wrong?" Plummey called.

"No, nothing," the Major cried. "Lead her to the right! There's a sunken log ahead, and she's got it on her mind. Turn her head a little more so she'll slide on past. A little more! There, that's the lad. Now try to hold her in quiet water till she tires."

Plummey leaned against a rock, crushing the reel seat against his chest. He wasn't tired, but for a moment his thoughts left the fish. He was remembering Betty Carlson and wishing she were there to watch.

The Major was having daydreams of his own. Mushrat John sat on a rock above the Great Pool, and behind him the Major saw his Uncle Mac. They both smiled at the Major and cast him invisible flies by way of greeting. He wished they would stick around awhile so he could show them off to Belle, or so he could take them on a tour of his stream. But they had a way of vanishing whenever he tried to bring them into focus.

The Queen fluttered near the surface of the pool and splashed water on both the Major and Plummey. The Major could see a spot on the line above the leader where a sharp rock, perhaps, had frayed it, but with luck it might hold. Plummey looked at him shyly, then looked down at his worn sneakers. His bare toes were visible through the canvas.

"Keep it up, son. Keep going. You've done a fine job. You don't know what a fish you've got there. You land her, and I'll see to it you go down in the record books. I'll be witness. So far you've fought a splendid fight; you deserve to finish!" The Major's voice trailed off almost to a sob.

Plummey brought the exhausted Queen up into the shallows finally, where she lay on her side, her gill covers working hard. Silently, the Major offered his net, but Plummey shook his head. So bright and beautiful! A record brookie! Major Quillaine himself had witnessed it. He could hardly wait to tell Mr. Sluter.

He glanced at the fish once more. There was a small slit along the cartilage of the jaw where a hook might have rusted out. His hook maybe.

The Major patted him on the back. "Congratulations, son," he said quietly.

Plummey reached down, wet his hands, took the heavy trout around the gill covers, and unhooked the fly. It was only a few quick steps to the screens that separated the Major's stream from the Deschutes. As the Major stared in amazement, Plummey staggered along, packing the dripping trout, then gently lowered her into the stream and let the current bathe her rosy gills. She looked so much more beautiful in the water. For some moments he steadied her as she gulped for oxygen. When, finally, he took his hand away, the fish lazed there as though taking her bearings. Then, slowly, wearily, she began to make her way up the Major's stream.

"Reminds me of a brookie I caught once up in Wood Buffalo Park in the Territories," the Major said as he traipsed upstream beside Plummey to wait for the Queen at her favorite pool. "It was—" the Major's voice hesitated a little then went on "—smaller than yours."

The Major peeled off his chest waders and sat on the rocks, letting his trousers steam in the warm spring sunshine.

"I know where we can find her a good mate," the Major said. "Keep her from getting lonely this fall when she's ready to spawn."

Upstream, a hatch of black drakes was creating a spectacle, and not far from the stream, green and scarlet black-chinned humming birds were busy in Belle's flowers. From high atop Plummey's cottonwood, a Bullock's oriole was singing out a territory.

Together they watched the Virgin Queen as she made her way up the riffles into her pool, swimming slowly, exploring each current with her nose. For some time, she lay in full view, ignoring the drifting hatch over her head, then, at last, she rose lazily and gulped a splendid drake. She was home.

From somewhere back toward the house, the Major heard Belle's voice calling him. He stood up and waved to her. She had old Sluter by the arm and was leading him across the field. A picnic basket, was draped from the other arm. He heard the peal of her silvery laughter, high-pitched, joyous as a bird's. Perhaps she had already guessed that he was not alone and the boy was sitting at his side.

The last golden cottonwood leaf had tumbled from Plummey's tree, exposing an oriole's silver nest against a November sky, when Major Quillaine came bustling out the back door of Mr. Sluter's house to the practice casting area, interrupting Plummey who was teaching Betty Carlson the fine points of making a mayfly dance.

"Am I ready for the river yet?" Betty teased as her fly did a nuptial waltz and floated down into a paper cup.

"Nice." The Major beamed. "Reminds me of a cast I made once on Henry's Fork, but I'll tell you about that later. Right now I want you kids to come with me over to my stream."

The Major looked tired. He had driven all night from Idaho and sported the start of a snow white beard, but a fierce excitement burned within and he hardly gave them time to put their rods away.

As they approached the horseshoe pool, they saw the water in the riffles boil and caught a flash of color as the Queen turned on her side, throwing up bottom gravel into the current.

"She's building a redd," Plummey said. "A place to lay her eggs!"

"Look behind her," the Major whispered.

"Wow!" Plummey exclaimed. "Hey, Betty! Look at the size of that brookie male! He's beautiful!"

The Queen was not impressed. Time and again she attacked the stranger and drove him away from her nest, returning always to her work digging out a scoop in the river gravels.

When Belle came out to join them, the sun was sinking lower above the Cascades, and the Queen seemed a little less belligerent. As darkness fell, a chill descended along the Pittock Bottom, a wind rattled the bare branches of the cottonwoods, and Betty's hands crept to Plummey's for warmth.

Plash! Plash!

"Listen!" the Major whispered, putting his arm around his wife's shoulders.

"Listen!" Plummey said, daring to put his arm around Betty's waist.

Plash! Plash! The sounds again almost in unison.

In the faint afterlight, they could glimpse the ripples of a double rise. The Queen and the great new brookie male were feeding side by side.